Is Meredith's life in danger?

She was shouting now, crowding Meredith back against the railing, gripping her elbows. The cold metal pushed into Meredith's spine. There was a sheer drop on this side of the path, down into a dark ravine tangled with vines and saplings and sharp with broken rocks . . .

Poison Pen

Mary Towne

10 9 8 7 6 5 4 3 2 1

CHAPTER 1

"Oh, no!" Corky stopped short in the classroom doorway. "Not old Graybags! What's she doing here? I thought she retired."

Meredith looked at her new friend in surprise. With her springy red curls and bubbly personality, Corky was well nicknamed. Usually she brimmed with friendliness and high spirits—undoubtedly the reason she'd been assigned by Mrs. Norman, their regular homeroom teacher, to show Meredith the ropes during her first weeks at La Playa Middle School.

"We had her in fourth grade," Corky muttered, dumping her books on the table she and Meredith shared with two other girls. "She expects you to be just about perfect, and she grades really hard."

Meredith studied the woman standing by the blackboard with her arms folded, waiting for the class to assemble. She wasn't young and blond and pretty like Mrs. Norman, but Meredith thought she looked pleasant enough—tanned and athletic-looking, like so many of the older people here in San Diego. She had short, silvery hair brushed back from a square forehead, and her clear blue eyes were almost the same vivid shade as Meredith's own.

As the bell rang, Emily Yamada slid into the chair next to Meredith's and whispered breathlessly, "Did you hear about Mrs. Norman? Oh, I hope she doesn't lose the baby!"

Mrs. Norman was six months pregnant with her first child. One of their class projects was researching names for the baby—not just making lists, but finding out where all the hundreds of names had come from and what they meant and who in history had had them. Mrs. Norman had warned them with a smile, though, that her husband was pretty much set on Bill for a boy and Laura for a girl.

Before Meredith could ask Emily what she meant, Ms. Gray—she'd written her name on the board—stepped forward and raised a hand for silence. Meredith was impressed at how quickly everyone quieted down.

"Well, now," she said briskly, "I think most of you know who I am, and of course I remember many of you from two years ago. Though I do see some unfamiliar faces. I'm looking forward to getting acquainted with you new people," she added with a smile that included Meredith and the handful of other new kids. "More about that later. But first I'd better explain why I'm here."

Corky said something under her breath, doodling a picture on the back of a notebook. But as Ms. Gray paused, she looked up and sat still, suddenly attentive like the rest of the class.

"As you know, Mrs. Norman had planned to continue teaching until Christmas vacation. Now I'm afraid that won't be possible. She had a fall on Saturday morning that resulted in a broken wrist and some bad bruises. She spent the weekend in the hospital, and although the baby's all right, her doctor wants her to take things easy from now on."

Ms. Gray stopped to let them absorb this, waiting for the exclamations of surprise and dismay to die down. Then she said quietly, "In any case, I doubt she'd want to return to this homeroom under the circumstances."

Noah Wright waggled his hand in the air. "Are you going to be our teacher now, Ms. Gray?" he asked. Noah always talked more than he listened.

Everyone else, though, had heard that strange last sentence. They stared at Ms. Gray.

She sighed. "Yes, Noah, I am, at least until other arrangements can be made." She smiled suddenly, wrinkles fanning out around her blue eyes. "Here I thought I'd earned an honorable discharge— nothing to do but play tennis all day and serve tea from my elegant set of retirement china."

"'Under the circumstances,'" Jeff Barlow repeated slowly from his seat at the front of the room. "What does that mean, Ms. Gray?"

Ms. Gray didn't answer right away. For a moment, she stood gazing out at the sunny October morning beyond the windows. When she turned back to the class, her expression was grim.

"I have Carol's—Mrs. Norman's—permission to tell you this," she said, "although it was given reluctantly. Her accident was the result of an unpleasant shock, in the form of an anonymous letter. She was halfway up the stairs to her apartment when she opened it. The shock was all the greater because the letter appears to have been sent by one of her own students—by someone in this class."

There was a moment of stunned silence, then a babble of outrage and bewilderment. Meredith shared the sense of astonishment. Who would do such a thing to Mrs. Norman? Even without Corky's telling her repeatedly how lucky they were to be in Mrs. Norman's sixth grade, it hadn't taken Meredith long to realize she was one of the most popular teachers in school. Why would anyone want to scare Mrs. Norman or hurt her feelings, or whatever the letter writer had done?

"How do you know?" Sara Freeman demanded belligerently, a scowl drawing her heavy brows together. "I mean, how do you know it was one of us?"

"Yeah," said Adam Kowalski from the back of the room, wide awake for once, leaning forward with his fists clenched on his heavy thighs. "Like Mrs. Norman recognized the handwriting or something?"

"There was no handwriting," Ms. Gray told them. "Just words and letters cut from magazines and newspapers and glued to a sheet of paper. And a picture—a very upsetting picture."

She shook her head. "I'll say no more about the contents. One of you knows exactly what they were. And one of you owes Mrs. Norman a heartfelt apology. At least I'd like to think it would come from the heart—that the letter was only a prank, and that the sender had no idea of the harm it might cause."

Again there was a frozen silence, but a different

kind of silence this time, with no one quite looking at anyone else.

"The letter Mrs. Reilly got," Jeff said suddenly. "Was it like that?"

Someone laughed, and Meredith saw several kids grinning in spite of themselves. She looked around blankly. Who was Mrs. Reilly? she wondered.

"But that was last year," Connie Morales objected. "In the spring."

Ms. Gray said, "We have no way of comparing the two letters, since Mrs. Reilly threw hers away." Again there were titters; she frowned at the offenders. "But yes, it does look as if the sender might be the same person."

"Wow!" Noah exclaimed, flopping back in his chair. "You mean like one of those poison pen deals? Right here in *school*?" Meredith saw him remember what Ms. Gray had said about their homeroom. He twisted around to stare at the kids behind him, then faced front again, open-mouthed. "But hey, it wouldn't be one of us! I mean, it just couldn't be."

When Ms. Gray didn't say anything, he protested, "And anyway, that other letter was funny, you know? Not mean or nasty, or whatever this one was like."

"It wasn't so funny to Mrs. Reilly," Ms. Gray said sharply. "Or to Mr. Reilly, either."

Reilly—the name finally rang a bell with Meredith. Wasn't Mr. Reilly the head custodian? Yes, the nice old guy with the red face who was always kidding around.

Emily Yamada said, frowning beneath her glossy black bangs, "You still haven't told us why you think it's someone in this class."

"No," said Ms. Gray, "and I'm not going to. I don't want to go into the details. Let's just say there's internal evidence, if anyone knows what that is."

Several kids nodded uncertainly, but she didn't explain further.

"As I mentioned, the person who sent the letter knows what it said. I imagine he or she must be feeling pretty sorry and ashamed right now, and is wondering how to make amends. A phone call to me or to the Normans will be kept confidential. I promise. So will a letter—a *real* letter, I mean—of apology."

She hesitated. "One other thing, class. If you could keep this to yourselves, I know Mrs. Norman would appreciate it. The incident was upsetting enough without having the whole school hear about it."

There was a respectful murmur of agreement. Meredith looked at Noah. She also glanced at Deirdre Loomis and several other girls and decided she wouldn't take any bets on the news not spreading through school by lunchtime.

"Very well," Ms. Gray said with a nod. She lifted a stack of worksheets from her desk. "Let's try to put all this behind us now and get down to business on the folklore unit you've been studying. Connie and Jeff, would you pass these out, please? And Adam, you might close those blinds behind you. I see the air conditioning in this wing doesn't work any better than it ever did."

She stopped while a jet roared by overhead, rattling the windowpanes, and added with a grimace, "Nor has the navy changed its flight pattern, I'm sorry to hear."

As the class settled down, shuffling books and papers and hunting for pens, Corky nudged Meredith and whispered, "Wait'll Ms. Gray finds out that Ron Selby's been bringing his baseball card collection to school and trading for extra desserts."

Meredith smiled but said, "How can she? He keeps it in his locker, except at lunchtime."

"She'll just know," Corky said darkly. "Just like she probably already knows I haven't even started the report I'm supposed to give on Wednesday about all those weird bird superstitions. Did you know some people believe if you cut your hair and a bird uses some of it to build a nest, you'll get a terrible headache?" She giggled. "Hey, maybe I'll bring my fingernail scissors to school and creep up behind old Graybags and *snip*—!"

"It's the wrong time of year for birds' nests," Meredith pointed out.

"Right." Corky sighed and uncapped her special pen—she was learning calligraphy. "And with any luck, she won't still be here in the spring."

Meredith had a feeling Corky's calligraphy was going to give Ms. Gray a headache, never mind fooling around with birds' nests, but she decided not to say so.

CHAPTER 2

When the bell rang for electives before lunch, Meredith expected everyone to start talking at once about the poison pen letters. But even when they were out in the corridor, beyond Ms. Gray's earshot, no one did. Some of the kids said how terrible it was about Mrs. Norman, and others agreed; mostly, though, they were quiet and subdued. Well, it must be a creepy feeling, Meredith thought, knowing that one of them was responsible for what had happened.

As they headed toward the music room in the opposite wing, she said curiously to Virginia Robb, a quiet blond girl who sat next to her in chorus, "What was in the other letter—the one last spring?"

Virginia shook her head. "I don't know. I'm new here, too, remember?"

Overhearing, Emily Yamada said, "Oh, that was about Mr. Reilly's lunches." She giggled. "Well, it really *was* kind of funny, except Mrs. Reilly's so nice, and I guess it hurt her feelings. She used to work in the cafeteria," she explained, "only she quit because of health food. Not having it, I mean."

Just ahead of them, Corky paused outside the door of the art room. "She kept trying to get them to stop serving stuff like pizza and cheeseburgers," she said with a grin, "only they wouldn't. So then she started up her own restaurant, this dinky little health-food place downtown, and she'd make special lunches for Mr. Reilly to bring to school. You know, like lentil sandwiches with bean sprouts in them."

"And salads with raw carrots and wheat germ," put in Connie Morales, catching up with them—she and Emily both sang alto in the chorus.

"And tofu, yuck!" said Emily, which made Meredith smile; evidently being Japanese American didn't mean you were born liking tofu. "And Mr. Reilly just *hated* them. He was always trying to trade with someone for a regular sandwich, a ham and cheese or a salami on rye or whatever. Everybody knew about it—it was a school joke, like: Who's going to get stuck with Mr. Reilly's spinach muffin today?"

Connie smiled but said, "Well, I guess Mrs. Reilly worries about him a lot. He had a heart attack a while back," she explained to Meredith and Virginia, "and he's supposed to be real careful about what he eats. You know, no whatever-it-is that messes up your arteries."

"Cholesterol," Corky supplied, a beat ahead of Meredith. Corky wasn't much of a reader, but she loved big words and always scored high on vocabulary tests.

Meredith nodded; her mother was careful about that kind of thing, too, though at least she let them choose their own school lunches. "But what about the letter?" she said. "I mean, what did it say?"

"Well, that was pretty much it," Emily said with a shrug. "About how Mr. Reilly was always trashing his special lunches. And there was a picture cut out of a newspaper showing this really gross fat man eating a banana split."

"No, a pie," Corky corrected her.

Connie said, "Yes, it must've been a picture about some pie-eating contest, because the guy had whipped cream and gunk smeared all over his face. It was really disgusting. And what the letter said was 'Is Your Husband Junking Himself to Death? Ask Him What He Does with Your Lunches.'"

"Mr. Reilly brought it to school to show the guys

he thought had done it," Emily explained. "Tommy Riegel and Steve Lopez and Keith Dunn—you know, the ones who think they're such hotshots and hang out around back of the shop at lunchtime. Mr. Reilly used to play poker with them sometimes, for peanuts." She laughed at Meredith's expression. "Really for peanuts, I mean, not money."

None of the names was familiar to Meredith, except for that of Keith Dunn, who was in her science class. And none of them was in Mrs. Norman's homeroom, she thought.

Corky said, "Mr. Reilly was really mad about the letter. He said his wife was so upset that she was ready to divorce him and let him stew in his own juices." She grinned, then looked sheepish. "Well, that's what he said."

"Only she never would," Emily said. "I mean, you'd have to know Mrs. Reilly. She's this really feisty little lady who's into stuff like conserving water and carpooling and recycling. Sometimes on weekends you'll see her in that park over on Miranda Street picking up trash with her grandchildren—these two little kids dragging a giant plastic bag around."

"So anyway," Connie finished the story, "now Mr. Reilly just buys stuff for lunch at the Seven-Eleven and eats by himself back in the utility room."

The second bell had rung while they were talking. Mr. Ramirez, the young art teacher, was holding the door open for Corky. Now he made her a sweeping bow and said, "Whenever you're ready, Ms. Edwards."

Corky flushed. Some of the kids teased her about having a crush on Mr. Ramirez, though Corky claimed the only reason she took art instead of chorus for her elective was that she couldn't carry a tune. Meredith thought it was also because her stepmother was an artist and Corky wanted to be one, too.

"Well, see you guys later," Corky said hastily, and added over her shoulder, "Hey, Merry, don't forget you're coming over for dinner tonight."

Meredith nodded but couldn't help sighing as the door closed after her. "I wish Corky would remember I hate being called Merry," she said.

"Try calling her Corinne," Emily advised with a grin.

"I'm the same way," Virginia confided unexpectedly to Meredith as they took their seats on the risers among the other second sopranos. "I can't stand it when people call me Ginny." She opened her music folder and added, "I think that's sort of sad about the Reillys, don't you?"

Meredith nodded. "Not just sad," she said thoughtfully. "Really—well, kind of poisonous."

CHAPTER 3

I've lived in California before—in fact, I was born in Long Beach, but I was only a baby when we moved away. Other states I've lived in are Virginia, Florida, Georgia, and Washington State. We also lived in the Phillipines when I was seven. Our last tour of duty was in Rhode Island. I forgot to say I'm a navy brat, but I guess you've figured that out. My dad is a sea-going officer (he just made captain!), that's why we move around so much.

"Just give me a page or two about yourself," Ms. Gray had told Meredith and the other new kids. "Whatever you feel like sharing with me. I'm sorry to do it this way, and of course I'll be scheduling conferences with each of you soon, but right now I have a lot of catching up to do."

Sitting at her beat-up desk by the window, Meredith frowned down at the shiny leaves of an avocado tree growing in the small side yard. The autobiography might not be a regular school assignment, but she had a feeling she'd better watch her spelling and punctuation anyway. Had she spelled "Phillipines" right?

She was reaching for her dictionary when her little brother Peter came pounding up the stairs into his room across the hall, followed by another grubby eight-year-old. Immediately they started wrestling, judging by all the thumps and giggles.

"Hey, keep it down," Meredith called, getting up to close her door. "I'm doing homework."

"Yes, *ma'am*!" Peter called back in a saluting tone of voice, but the noise subsided. He knew the rules. In a family of six, living in rented houses where space was often cramped, you learned to respect one another's privacy. At least here they each had their own bedroom, Meredith thought gratefully, remembering the room she'd shared with her sister Lindsay back in Newport—chaotic on one side (Lindsay's) and neat on the other (Meredith's), with an old bedspread slung over a clothesline to mark the division.

She crossed out one of the "l's" in "Phillipines" and added another "p." Then she continued:

I have an older brother, Dan, who's 17, a sister, Lindsay, 15, and a younger brother, Peter, 8. We get along pretty well. My father says we have to be like the crew of a ship and all pull together. I guess you could say my mom is like the first mate, only sometimes I think she's really the skipper (captain) because she's the one that gives most of the orders, even when my dad is home and not at sea. She's sort of strict, but fair. My dad is more easygoing and likes to kid around more.

A little like the difference between Mrs. Norman and Ms. Gray, Meredith found herself thinking. She felt guilty that she might end up liking Ms. Gray better as a teacher—guilty because of what had happened to Mrs. Norman. You couldn't help liking Mrs. Norman as a person, she was so pretty and cheerful and upbeat about everything. At least she had been until last weekend.

Meredith shivered in spite of the hot sunlight slanting across her desk. It was almost scary, thinking that someone in her class was capable of sending an anonymous letter. No matter what Ms. Gray said, it didn't sound as if the letter had been just a prank, not with all the work it must have involved.

She pushed the subject aside and returned her thoughts to the change of teachers. The truth was she'd been finding her schoolwork a little too easy so far—a little boring, in fact. This was partly because she'd already had some of the stuff they were learning in other schools, but partly, too, because Mrs. Norman was sort of casual about checking their work. As long as she thought you were doing your best, she was satisfied. But how did she know what someone's best really was? Did she try to find out? Meredith thought somehow that Ms. Gray would. She went on with her homework.

I like swimming and going for hikes and bike rides, also playing my flute. I'm not very good because of changing music teachers so much, but I have fun fooling around with it. I also love animals and learning about them. I think the zoo here in San Diego is one of the neatest places I've ever been.

What else? Ms. Gray had mentioned hobbies and special interests, but Meredith couldn't think of any, unless you counted reading. She loved to read. Practically the first thing she did when they moved to a new place was get a public library card. But she wouldn't mention that—it might sound as if she was trying to impress Ms. Gray in some phony way.

Deciding to see if she could get a few minutes on the computer in the family room, Meredith tore the page out of her notebook and headed for the stairs.

Peter had closed his door, but Meredith could hear that he was showing his beloved rock collection to his new friend—Eddy, was it, or Andy? She shook her head. Peter always had to have a best friend wherever they lived, and he was always heartbroken when the time came to say good-bye and follow the moving van to a new place. He didn't understand yet that it was better just to be friendly with other kids and not get too close to anyone in particular.

This reminded Meredith that she was supposed to be going over to Corky's house for dinner that night, for the third time in as many weeks. Well, Corky was a special case, she thought with a smile. Also, her household was a casual one—just her father, a lawyer who often worked late at his office, her stepmother, Paula, and the baby, Will. Paula was the kind of cook who either tossed something absentmindedly into the microwave or got adventurous and used every pot and pan in the kitchen. Tonight she was cooking Mexican, Corky had said, celebrating the start of a new series of paintings she was excited about.

Meredith figured there'd be a lot of dishes to wash afterward, but she didn't mind. She and Corky could play the radio full blast while they cleaned up, something she was rarely allowed to do at home. And maybe they could go for a swim later, if it didn't get too cold after the sun went down. The Edwards had an in-ground pool in their spacious backyard, big enough to swim laps in. It was carefully fenced because of Will, with a play area between the pool and the bathhouse that Mr. Edwards had converted into a studio for Paula, cutting a skylight in the roof and adding a big window on the north side.

The pool was one thing of Corky's Meredith really envied. She'd thought that, living in San Diego, they'd be near the beach, but rentals near the coast were really expensive—more than her father's housing allowance would stretch to, especially with four kids to accommodate. Instead, they'd taken a house several miles inland, in a pleasant but unexciting neighborhood of condos and single-family houses bordered by dry, brush-filled canyons, without even a distant view of the Pacific.

As Meredith cut through the kitchen to the family room, Dan and her mother came in the back door with a load of wallpaper books and some cans of paint. One thing about Mom, she insisted on fixing up each rental house as if she owned it and planned to live there forever—no dingy walls or scuffed baseboards for Joyce Harding. The right to redecorate had to be in the lease or she wouldn't sign.

Dan was looking grumpy. He'd had to leave his car behind in Rhode Island, an ancient Dodge their father said would never make it across the country. Now he and Mom were sharing the station wagon, with Dan helping her run errands at the base exchange at Miramar, the nearby naval air station. In return, he got to drive to school several days a week.

"There, I think that's everything," Mrs. Harding said in her checklist voice, and she turned to Meredith with a smile. "How was school, hon?" She was a small, trim woman with permed dark hair and lively brown eyes in a heart-shaped face.

"Okay," Meredith told her, then hesitated. Ms. Gray had asked them not to talk to outsiders about the poison pen thing, but did that include parents? She was used to sharing things, important things at least, with her parents, and she knew they'd be concerned. But anyway, now wasn't the moment.

She settled for saying, "We have a new homeroom teacher. Mrs. Norman fell and broke her wrist and has to take things easy for a while, so I guess she won't be coming back. Not till second semester, anyway."

Her mother's expression softened with instant sympathy. "Oh, what a shame. Is the baby all right?" When Meredith nodded, she said, "Well, it'll be a terrible bore, lying low for the next few months, but it'll be worth it in the end—she'll see."

Dan growled, "Hey, you mean even I was worth it? Me with my big feet and my big mouth and my habit of taking corners too fast?"

"Most of the time," his mother told him crisply. "Especially when you do nice things for me like bringing in the stepladder from the garage, so I can start taking down that tacky wallpaper in the front hall."

Dan sighed and let his shoulders sag dramatically, but threw Meredith a wink as he went out the door.

In the family room, Meredith found Lindsay sitting slumped at the worktable in front of the small PC, which was almost buried under piles of papers and books. The cursor on its half-filled screen looked somehow as if it had been blinking in the same place for a long time.

"No TV," Lindsay snapped over her shoulder at Meredith, looking around for her glasses and putting them on. "I've still got at least another hour to do on this stupid history paper."

"I just wanted to see if I could use the computer for about fifteen minutes," Meredith said mildly, holding up her single sheet of notebook paper.

Lindsay groaned, raked her fingers through her sandy hair, and pushed back her chair. "Oh, why not?" she said, jabbing at the keyboard to clear the screen. "What do I care about the French Revolution? I'm never going to be asked who Robespierre was when I'm adjusting the mix on a turbine or straightening out a crankshaft."

Of all of them, Lindsay had the hardest time functioning as a member of a crew, being naturally impatient and messy. Ironically, she was also the only one who wanted to follow their father and pursue a career in the navy. She kidded that it was because of all the guys she'd be able to meet, but she also had a passion for anything to do with nautical machinery.

"Hey, you're going over to the Edwards' tonight,

aren't you?" she asked. Meredith nodded. "Well, be sure and tell them I'm available to baby-sit Will anytime they need me. I mean, as long as I don't have a date or something."

Meredith didn't have the heart to point out that Corky was usually available to take care of Will when Paula couldn't. But the fact was that dating hadn't taken up much of Lindsay's time as yet, in spite of efforts to watch her weight, keep her clothes in order, and refrain from arguing with boys who thought they knew more about carburetors than she did. Now she'd decided contact lenses were the answer, and she was doing all the baby-sitting she could to earn money for them.

Meredith knew that she herself had received more than her fair share of the family's good looks. Dan and she had the same straight, glossy dark hair and regular features, but his eyes were brown like their mother's, while hers were cobalt blue like Dad's. She also knew that her looks often drew people to her, at least as long as she was careful to smile a lot and seem interested in whatever they were doing or saying. Otherwise, she could appear sort of aloof, even snooty.

She didn't think she was either—but there were times at school when she wished she could just forget about other people and act the way she felt.

Other kids could yawn if they got bored or scowl if they were in a bad mood or just go off by themselves if they needed some private space. But when you were always the new girl, and pretty besides—

With a sigh, Meredith sat down at the computer, moved Lindsay's can of Diet Coke a safer distance from the keyboard, and began typing her auto-biography.

CHAPTER 4

"Whew, I should've remembered to do this the other way around," Corky said, pushing the stroller up the hill. "Down into Bear Canyon, not up. Let's get a soda before we do the elephants, okay? And maybe some juice for Will. There's a stand up at the top, over near the colobus monkeys."

"Okay, but I'm paying," Meredith said firmly. This was the second time she'd been to the zoo as Corky's guest, using one of the free passes that came with the Edwards' zoo membership. She'd tried to pay her own way today, even though the ticket would have used up most of her remaining October allowance, but Corky wouldn't hear of it.

They emerged from the shade of tall eucalyptus trees onto the zoo's sunny main level, crowded on this crisp Saturday morning with visitors of all ages, colors, and nationalities.

"The best time to come is on a weekday," Corky observed. "First thing in the morning, when there's hardly anyone around. 'Course that's when you get the crazies, too."

"Crazies?"

"You know—people who sort of hang out here. Like some of them have pet names for the animals, and they talk to them and even sing to them." Corky giggled. "One time there was a guy playing a harmonica inside the reptile house, like he thought he was a snake-charmer or something. Hey, Merry, you should bring your flute sometime and see if it really works."

Meredith made a face—partly because she had no intention of ever going inside the reptile house if she could help it, partly because Corky was calling her Merry again.

They got their sodas and started slowly around the oval perimeter of the elephant exhibit.

"Oh, hey, remind me to get some flashbulbs," Corky said as they passed a group of tourists snapping pictures. "Maybe Paula could stop somewhere on the way home. For Monday," she explained, when Meredith looked at her blankly. "You know, the senior citizen thing."

Ms. Gray was starting them on an oral history project, interviewing longtime residents of San Diego for their recollections of the city's past. She'd divided the class into three research teams and assigned each team a neighborhood adjoining the school. They'd be putting together a scrapbook to go with their report—pictures of the people they talked to and of any mementos they might have. Corky had been appointed the artist/photographer for Meredith's team.

Meredith said, "I've never done anything like that before. It sounds like it might be sort of fun."

"Oh, it's gonna be neat," Corky said enthusiastically. "Even old Graybags has a good idea once in a while. I mean, this way we get to *go* places, right? A whole lot better than being stuck in the library looking up names."

The first-name project had been gradually phased out. They'd printed up a report of the information they'd collected and sent it to Mrs. Norman, along with a card they'd all signed. She'd written the class a cheerful thank-you note saying she was feeling fine, was learning to knit, and would see them next semester. Even Corky now seemed resigned to the change of teachers, though Meredith wished she wouldn't keep referring to Ms. Gray as Graybags.

As they rounded the elephant barn, Will said something that sounded like "horsie" and twisted around in the stroller to look anxiously up at Corky. They saw he'd been watching a rhinoceros on the other side of the walkway, slowly pacing its rock-walled enclosure with ponderous shiftings of its armor-plated hide.

"Rhino, Will," Corky told him, and grinned. "Not exactly something you'd want to take a pony ride on."

Meredith was reading the plaque attached to the heavy fencing, marked with a big *E* for Endangered, when Corky exclaimed, "Hey, speak of the devil, sort of." She pointed. "Looks like half our research team is here."

Meredith looked where she was pointing and saw Jeff Barlow standing farther along the elephant fence with Noah Wright and another boy.

"Gosh, why does Jeff want to hang out with a dork like Noah?" Corky complained, then answered her own question with a laugh. "I bet that other kid is some relative of Noah's, and Jeff got himself invited along. That's mostly when kids here get to come to the zoo," she added. "When they have out-of-town company."

She wheeled the stroller toward the boys, who were watching the smallest of the elephants lower itself into the pool at the edge of the enclosure. It wallowed for a moment, then sucked up a trunkful of water and sprayed it over its high-domed head and wrinkled shoulders, exactly like a human taking a shower. Will crowed with delight.

"Batteries," Corky said suddenly, snapping her fingers. "I better remind Noah to check the ones in his tape recorder for when we do our interviews. It'd be just like him to bring back a whole long tape full of nothing."

Meredith sighed resignedly. Corky was always minding other people's business.

While Corky buttonholed Noah, Jeff turned to Meredith with a smile that lightened his rather serious features and warmed his brown eyes. "Hi, Merry. Some scene, right?"

"I'd come here every day if I could," she agreed shyly—something about Jeff always made her feel slightly breathless. But she couldn't help adding, "Please don't call me Merry, though."

Jeff looked surprised. "Hey, sorry. I just always hear Corky calling you that."

"I know," she said ruefully. "I can't get her to stop."

"Well, you know Corky—always take a shortcut if you can. Meredith being kind of a long name," he explained. "I think it's pretty, though."

While Meredith was trying to think of something to say—"thank you" didn't seem quite right, since she hadn't chosen the name herself—Jeff looked over at Noah and said with a grin, "I trust you've got your pencil all sharpened for Monday morning."

Meredith was the official notetaker for their team—Ms. Gray said there were details you could capture only in writing, never mind photos and recorders—while Jeff and Pete Sanchez were in charge of preparing the interview questions. Ms. Gray didn't believe in leaving much to chance.

They moved aside to let one of the zoo trams go by, the driver intoning facts about elephants through her microphone.

Jeff said, "Hey, you know who else is here today? Mr. Norman. I saw him parking his motorcycle out in the lot. Oh, that's right, you probably never met him. He's a real character—plays trumpet in a jazz band and surfs whenever he can. See him zooming around on his motorcycle and you'd never guess he's a teacher, too. Special ed over in PB, where he can catch a wave or two at lunchtime."

PB was Pacific Beach, Meredith had learned, one of the beach communities where her father had gone house hunting in vain.

"Anyway, he said Mrs. Norman is doing fine, and the baby's still due right on schedule—Bill or Laura."

Meredith smiled, but said, "Did he say anything about the poison pen letter? I mean, did they ever find out who sent it?" Ms. Gray hadn't referred to the matter again.

"I didn't want to ask him. I guess at least she hasn't gotten any more of them."

"Maybe whoever it was really did learn a lesson."

Jeff considered this for a moment, then shook his head. "I don't know—I think the person has gotta be sort of sick, don't you? I mean, someone with real problems."

Meredith could think of several kids in their homeroom who were definitely on the weird side, but since Jeff didn't mention any names, neither did she.

They'd wandered back to the start of the elephant exhibit as they talked. Jeff looked over at the colobus monkeys and said, "Hey, wouldn't it be great to have a monkey for a pet?" He grinned. "Well, maybe not one with such a long tail—I can just hear my mom on that subject. I already talked her into a guinea pig and a rabbit and a parrot," he explained, "and we just live in a condo. Do you have any pets?"

"Not right now. We used to have an English sheepdog, Tuffy, but he got old and sick and we had to have him put down."

That had been three years ago, but Meredith's eyes still stung at the memory. She turned her head away so Jeff wouldn't see.

"And for a while we had cats, but it's hard moving around with cats. They don't like new places, and they were always running away and getting lost."

"It must be rough," Jeff said. "Moving so much, I mean. We've only moved once, from Michigan when I was six, and I hope we never have to again. The only thing I really miss is ice-skating. Not that I was exactly a star on ice when I was six," he allowed with a smile, "but I think I would've liked playing hockey."

Having seen Jeff's speed and agility on the soccer field, Meredith thought he would have been good at it, too.

"Do you think maybe you might get to stay here in San Diego?" he asked after a pause. "I mean, a lot of navy people seem to live here sort of permanently."

People with shore jobs, Meredith thought. But her father would never put in for a shore appointment, if only because that would probably mean the end of any real advancement in the service. She shrugged and said, "It'd be nice. But it's fun traveling around and getting to see new places, too."

Jeff looked dubious. "Well, traveling, sure. But I guess I'd always want to have the same place to come home to. You know, with the same friends and everything. Even Noah," he added with a sigh. "Would you believe Noah's cousin is even more of a dweeb than he is? He wanted to hang out playing video games today instead of coming to the zoo. I mean, the guy lives in Utah, and this place is world-famous! Me, I come here every chance I get."

"Same here," Meredith agreed.

She was already planning to ask Paula how much a family membership cost. When you considered that there were six of them to use it, how expensive could it be? And if she had a free pass, she surprised herself by thinking, maybe she could invite Jeff to use it sometime.

CHAPTER 5

"What were you and Jeff talking about all that time?" Corky asked as they headed back with the stroller toward the gift shops and the exit. Paula was picking them up at eleven-thirty.

"Oh . . . just stuff."

"Well, you better watch it," Corky told her. "Jeff's who I picked out to be my boyfriend two years from now. I don't plan on dating till then," she explained. "Too much other stuff to do."

Meredith smiled, thinking she was kidding, then looked at her face and wasn't so sure. For all her sparkling hazel-green eyes and sunny smile, Corky had a very determined jaw.

"Oh, hey," Corky said, glancing at the big clock near the entrance, "we've still got five minutes. Do you mind watching Will while I run and check the gorillas one more time? I want to see if the new baby is outside now that it's warmed up some."

Meredith shook her head that no, she didn't mind, and Corky sped off, weaving nimbly through the crowd in her jeans and Padres sweatshirt, her bright hair bouncing.

Corky was fascinated by the gorillas, but Meredith always felt uncomfortable about watching them for any length of time. She knew it was good for people to see the gorillas and learn about them, also that most of the animals had been born in captivity and had no memory of their native forests, so different from this dry, sunny landscape on the shores of the Pacific. But even in their spacious new state-of-the-art exhibit, there was something both dignified and forlorn about the great apes that tugged at Meredith's heart.

"I hate it when people point at the gorillas and laugh at them," Corky had said fiercely, and Meredith knew what she meant. They agreed on that much at least.

"So how's everything at the zoo?" Paula inquired as Corky settled Will into his car seat. She glanced at the rearview mirror and tucked some stray hairs under the flowered cotton bandeau that held her smooth brown ponytail in place. Paula hated air conditioning and always drove with the car windows wide open.

"I've been by here three times," she added pointedly, "enjoying a lovely tour of the parking lot. I know, I know—just one more look at the gorillas, right?"

"Oh, but you should see the baby," Corky told her. "His name is Moke, and he's so *cute*."

Paula smiled and shook her head. As Meredith got into the passenger seat, leaving Corky to ride in back with Will, she thought how lucky Corky was to have a stepmother like Paula—not only young and talented and as pretty as a fashion model, but also funny and nice.

Corky thought so, too. "I'd rather have a big sister than a mother any day," she'd said. "'Course, *your* mom is really great," she'd added quickly, "even if she does have all those rules and schedules and things. Well, I guess she needs them, there are so many of you." Meredith had smiled to herself, thinking that Corky would make an even more unruly crew member than her sister Lindsay.

Corky's own mother had taken off when Corky was four, to join a women's commune in New Mexico. "Taken off"—that was how Corky put it, sounding casual, as if it were such ancient history

41

that it didn't matter anymore.

"She was really young when she and Dad got married," Corky had explained with a shrug. "And then I came along, and I guess she felt sort of trapped. You know, like she'd never had time to find out who she really was and what she wanted to do in life."

When Meredith frowned, she'd said, "Hey, it happens. And she knew my dad would do his best for me."

Meredith had only met Mr. Edwards a couple of times, but he'd struck her as a rather tense, preoccupied sort of man—not the kind of father who'd have been apt to give a four-year-old much in the way of hugs or bedtime stories. Of course, she hadn't said that; instead, she'd asked, "Do you ever hear from her—your mother?"

Corky shook her head. "We got some postcards at first. But then she left the commune after she and Dad got divorced, and we stopped hearing anything. We don't even know where she is now. Though I think maybe my grandmother does."

She laughed suddenly. "Now *that* was an ugly time, when my grandmother came to live with us. I guess she thought it was her duty or something. She stuck it out for about two years, and then she went back to Phoenix and her bridge club and her jazzercise classes. Wait, I've got a picture somewhere."

They'd been in Corky's room at the time. She'd rummaged in a dresser drawer and handed Meredith a photograph of a thin, dressy-looking lady wearing a pink suit and tinted glasses with decorated frames. Meredith wondered what Corky's mother looked like, but if Corky had a picture of her, too, she didn't offer to show it.

"Listen, I'm a whole lot better off without them," Corky had told her, tossing the photo back into the drawer. "My mother and my grandmother, both. I mean, if they'd stuck around, Dad would never have met Paula, and there wouldn't be any Will, and I wouldn't have the great life I have. Believe me, I don't spend any time crying over my poor, mixed-up mother. Good riddance is the way I look at it."

Now, as Paula maneuvered the car through the Saturday morning traffic onto the freeway, Meredith thought that Corky was probably right. Both her mother and her grandmother sounded like selfish types, and certainly there was no doubting how happy Mr. Edwards was with Paula, the way his face lit up whenever she came into a room.

"I need to stop and pick up some groceries," Paula told them once they were off the freeway again and halted at a red light. "Can you come have a bite of lunch with us, Meredith? Or I could drop you off first if you want."

"Thanks, but I think I'd better get home," Meredith said, aware of the number of meals she'd already eaten at the Edwards', also that it was her Saturday to do the vacuuming. Actually it was Lindsay's turn, but they'd traded because Lindsay had a date tonight with a boy she'd met while flying a kite with Peter in Mission Bay Park. He'd been running along one of the tracks when Lindsay crashed into him, backing up to reel in string. It was only the third date Lindsay had ever had, and she planned to spend the whole afternoon getting ready for it.

Meredith didn't mention the vacuuming, though, knowing Corky and Paula would only kid her. Housecleaning was a haphazard affair at the Edwards', usually delayed until Mr. Edwards remarked mildly that he could no longer find his slippers for all the dust bunnies under the bed.

As Paula turned onto the winding street that led to Meredith's house, she had to swerve sharply to avoid a kid on a skateboard.

"Tim McDermott," Corky said from the back seat. Meredith recognized him belatedly as a boy in their homeroom. "Hey, he's getting pretty good," Corky added, turning to watch the boy swoop lithely from curb to roadway and back again.

"Well, I wish he'd practice somewhere safer," Paula said. "Good thing I was going slowly."

"Tim's a whole lot better since Kevin Porter moved to L.A.," Corky informed Meredith. "Better in the way he acts, I mean. He and Kevin were always getting in trouble together," she explained. "Like last year they were into graffiti, sneaking around with cans of spray paint and writing this really crude stuff on people's garage doors. Kevin was sort of mean, but Tim's not too bad once you get to know him."

Meredith had to take this on faith, since she'd barely exchanged two words with Tim. She realized that the boys she tended to notice were the ones Jeff Barlow hung out with. Somehow she always knew where Jeff was and what he was doing, almost without having to look. It had something to do with the back of his head, she thought vaguely—with the way his hair grew there.

"Hey, wake up," Corky said, and Meredith gave a start. But Corky was talking to Will, who was nodding in his car seat with his thumb in his mouth. "Store, Will. Lobsters!"

"Lobsters?" Meredith echoed as Will opened his eyes.

Corky giggled. "You know the ones they keep in a tank near the fish counter, all tangled up together? Will's sort of scared of them, but as long as I hold his hand, he likes to go look at them."

Meredith laughed. She knew exactly how Will felt. She didn't like creepy, crawly things, either. She thought of the reptile house at the zoo. Maybe if she had someone to hold her hand, though—the right someone . . .

CHAPTER 6

"Sit down, Meredith." Ms. Gray indicated a chair across the table in the small teacher's room she was using for student conferences.

"Well, now, how are you liking San Diego so far? Apart from the zoo, that is," she added with a smile, glancing down at Meredith's neatly printed autobiography on top of the folder in front of her.

"It seems very nice," Meredith said politely. "I like the way everything's so clean and modern, compared with some of the places we've lived. And it's neat to have it be so warm and sunny all the time, but cool in the shade."

"Yes, it's a wonderful climate," Ms. Gray agreed. She looked at Meredith thoughtfully. "What would you say is your favorite of all the places you've lived so far?"

Meredith shook her head. "I don't really have one. I mean, they've all been different. Anyway, it's better not to have a favorite place, so you won't miss it too much when you have to leave."

"So home is really where your family is—the tight ship?"

Meredith nodded, feeling herself go tense inside. She didn't like adults feeling sorry for her, as if her parents were doing something wrong in not giving her a regular home with an address that stayed the same from year to year. She loved her dad and was proud of him, and if his navy career meant they had to move around a lot, well, that was just the way things were.

But Ms. Gray said only, "You're lucky to have a ship like that in this day and age. A lot of the families I see are more like leaky rowboats." As Meredith smiled, Ms. Gray consulted the autobiography again. "I see you play the flute. Have you thought of trying out for the band? I know Mr. Jessop would love to have you—he's always looking for woodwinds."

"I decided to take chorus instead," Meredith told her. "The last school I went to didn't have a band, so I'm kind of out of practice." She shrugged.

"Anyway, I like singing, and chorus is a good way to get to know kids."

"Yes, I notice you've already made some friends. Corky, of course, and Emily Yamada—would you believe I taught Emily's father?—and Virginia Robb."

"Emily's nice," Meredith agreed, "but I don't know Virginia too well. And Corky was sort of assigned to me." She grinned. "It's not exactly hard to be friends with Corky. But usually I get along with other kids pretty well."

Ms. Gray said, "Did you know Virginia's a great hiker and camper? She and her family backpacked down into the Grand Canyon last summer, on their way here from Indiana, and I know she's already done some long bike rides in this area."

"Really?" Meredith hadn't even known where Virginia was from, except that it was somewhere in the Midwest. She was guiltily aware that the reason she hadn't tried to get to know Virginia better was that she, too, was new in school. Meredith had learned from experience that it was a mistake to hang out with other new kids—it just delayed fitting in with the ones who already belonged.

"Well, now, let's talk about your schoolwork for a moment." Ms. Gray opened the folder and ran her eyes over some notes she'd made. "In general, I'm very pleased, Meredith—good, careful work that tells me you do plenty of preparation at home. The only area you seem to be rather weak in is geography. World geography, that is," she said with a smile. "I'm sure you must know the map of the United States by heart. And in math—"

There was a sudden rap at the door. Ms. Gray looked surprised, but got up to open it.

"I'm sorry to disturb you, Katherine, but I need a word with you." It was Mr. Bernstein, the curly-haired young vice principal, looking unusually grave about something.

Ms. Gray hesitated, then said, "Excuse me, Meredith. I'll be with you in a minute."

She closed the door behind her. Meredith heard a few terse sentences in Mr. Bernstein's bass rumble, followed by a sharp exclamation from Ms. Gray. Had Mr. Bernstein caught someone smoking or drinking beer on the school grounds? But why would he bother Ms. Gray about something like that?

The minute became two, then five. There was no longer any sound from the corridor, only a faint clatter of pots and pans and silverware from the cafeteria a few doors down—it was the period before lunch. Meredith's stomach growled. As the clock clicked off another minute, she began to feel trapped in this cell-like little room, whose cement-block walls were bare except for the clock and a Sierra Club calendar hanging open to the month of October.

At least there was a window, a small one above the chair where Ms. Gray had been sitting. Meredith edged around the table, resisting the temptation to peek at her folder lying there, and found herself looking out at the wide, grassy courtyard that separated the cafeteria wing from the gym beyond.

A car was drawn up by the gym's side door. Meredith squinted at it and recognized the beat-up blue Saab belonging to Ms. Carasso, one of the gym teachers. In the next moment, she also recognized Ms. Gray's white cardigan sweater as she stood leaning through the passenger window, talking to someone inside. As Meredith watched, Ms. Gray straightened, gave a brief nod, and thrust something into the pocket of her skirt.

The car pulled away fast, almost spinning its tires. Ms. Gray stood looking after it for a long moment, then turned back onto the walkway that bisected the courtyard. Her stride had none of its usual spring.

Mystified, Meredith returned to her chair. Had Ms. Carasso been in an accident or something? But the car hadn't looked any worse than usual. Maybe her little girl was sick or hurt. Meredith hoped not— she was a really cute kid who sometimes spent afternoons playing in the gym office when her preschool was over for the day.

"Sorry about that, Meredith."

Ms. Gray reentered the room briskly, leaving the door open this time. As she sat down, she slid something into the briefcase beside her chair—an envelope, Meredith thought it was. She picked up Meredith's folder and said, "Now where were we?"

Meredith saw that her hands were trembling slightly.

"Is everything all right?" she found herself asking.

"Oh"—Ms. Gray shrugged—"just a problem one of the other teachers wanted to discuss. I've been here so long that everyone expects me to play Mother whenever there's any kind of upset." She gave Meredith a smile that didn't quite reach her eyes. "Teachers are people, too, you know."

But Meredith was sure this wasn't any ordinary upset. She looked down at the briefcase, then back at Ms. Gray's strained face.

"There's been another one, hasn't there?" she said slowly. "Another poison pen letter." Before Ms. Gray could respond, she explained, "I didn't mean to be snooping or anything, but I was looking out the window just now, and . . . It's Ms. Carasso, isn't it? She got one."

CHAPTER 7

Ms. Gray sat back in her chair and blew out her breath in an angry sigh. "I'm afraid so," she said. "It came in the mail yesterday."

"But *why*? I mean, why Ms. Carasso?"

Ms. Carasso wasn't just an ordinary gym teacher, she was also the soccer coach—a pretty, vigorous young woman with a mane of streaky blond hair. She had a voice that could shatter glass at fifty yards but that could also give way to sudden, infectious laughter. Meredith had never heard anyone say a word against her. Even the boys bragged that Ms. Carasso could coach circles around any of the male soccer coaches at neighboring schools.

"Why, indeed?" Ms. Gray shook her head. "Just about the last person you'd expect to be the target of someone's malice. But then you could say the same thing about the Reillys and Mrs. Norman."

"Is she going to quit—Ms. Carasso?"

"No, though she was certainly tempted. Right now she's more angry than anything else. She's taking the day off to try to simmer down." Ms. Gray smiled faintly—Ms. Carasso's temper was famous—and then hesitated. "I hope I can trust you, Meredith, to say nothing of this to anyone." When Meredith nodded uncertainly, Ms. Gray explained, "Ms. Carasso doesn't want her letter made public—not even the fact that she received one. I think that's just as well, since I suspect the sender enjoys the publicity. It's a feeling of power, I suppose."

Meredith was silent, trying to digest this. Finally she said, "You're sure it's the same person? The same sender?"

Ms. Gray sighed again. "Unlike Mrs. Norman's letter, this one could have been sent by anyone in school—or out of it, for that matter. But yes, because it matches the others, I'm afraid we have to go on assuming the sender is someone in your class. My class." She grimaced.

"Matches it?"

"In the way it was put together—the photograph and the cut-out letters and so on. And also in its cruelty."

Meredith could smell chili dogs and potato salad being prepared in the cafeteria down the hall, but she no longer felt hungry. She said, "What about fingerprints? Don't they show up on paper?" Immediately she felt foolish, as if Ms. Gray might think she'd watched too many TV crime shows.

But Ms. Gray was nodding. "That's where Ms. Carasso was earlier this morning—at the police station, having the letter checked for prints. She was careful about handling it as soon as she realized what it was. Even so, the only clear prints on it were her own. Either the writer wore gloves or was careful to wipe the surfaces clean—the envelope as well as the letter itself."

The envelope . . . "What about the address?" Meredith asked. "Was that done with cut-out letters, too?"

"No. The address was typed—or rather printed out from a computer. Mrs. Norman's was done the same way, though she didn't think to save the envelope."

Meredith said excitedly, "Well, couldn't they trace that? I mean, not everyone has a computer, so that would narrow things down, at least. And then they could look for the same kind of printing that's on the envelope."

"Yes, we thought of that. Unfortunately, the

address was done with a laser printer, and I gather it's almost impossible to distinguish between one laser printer and another. As for access to a computer"—Ms. Gray shrugged—"almost everyone has that these days, even sixth graders, whether or not they have a computer at home."

"But a lot of people don't have laser printers," Meredith pointed out. Her own family's printer was an old-fashioned one with a typing wheel. "So that could still be a way of narrowing things down. The police could go to kids' houses, the ones who have computers, and—"

"I can see it's high time for our civics unit," Ms. Gray interrupted sharply, sounding for a moment like her normal classroom self. "The police couldn't do anything of the sort without a search warrant—luckily for all of us. And the same thing would be true of taking fingerprints, assuming we had any prints to match. They'd need a definite suspect first."

She gave Meredith a moment to think about this, then added, "In any event, there's a limit to what the authorities can do in a case like this, where no one's actually been threatened."

"Threatened?"

"If someone gets an anonymous letter saying that her life is in danger or that her house will be burned down," Ms. Gray explained, "the police will open an investigation. What's been happening here comes under the heading of harassment—hate mail. It's not all that uncommon, I'm sorry to say. The police can't possibly investigate every case that's reported to them."

"But Mrs. Norman could have lost her baby!" Meredith protested.

"I know. Yet the letter she received didn't threaten any injury or violence. All it did was ask a question—a particularly nasty question." Ms. Gray's blue eyes were somber, and there were lines around her mouth that Meredith had never noticed before.

"The letters," Meredith said suddenly. "I mean all the cut-out letters and words. Wouldn't the person doing this be saving up newspapers and magazines so they'd have plenty of headlines to choose from?"

"Possibly." Ms. Gray nodded. "Probably."

"Well, look, if I could get myself invited over to kids' houses, I could look in their closets, and maybe their basements and attics, too." Except most California houses didn't have either basements or attics, Meredith thought. And besides that . . . "I guess I'd never be able to do that with everyone in the class," she admitted. "But the police—" Again she stopped, remembering what Ms. Gray had said about search warrants.

Ms. Gray was smiling at her—a real smile this time. "I know you want to help, Meredith," she said gently. "But I don't see how you can. I've already involved you in a way I didn't intend. The most helpful thing you can do is to keep quiet about this latest episode."

"But I *want* to be involved," Meredith said, surprising herself with the force of her concern. "I mean, this stuff is really terrible! And what if the person does it again?"

Ms. Gray bowed her head. "I don't know," she admitted. "We just have to hope that when there's no reaction from Ms. Carasso, the letter writer will get bored and give up."

"And never get caught." Meredith frowned. "That's wrong." She slumped back in her chair, then straightened again as a new thought occurred to her. "I guess I'm not a suspect, am I?" As Ms. Gray looked startled, Meredith explained, "Well, I'm new this year, so I couldn't have written the letter to Mrs. Reilly. And the same goes for the other new kids. But everyone else in the class is a suspect, right?"

Ms. Gray nodded reluctantly.

"Well, then—" Meredith drew a deep breath. "I could be your watcher. Your spy, sort of. I don't mean in a sneaky kind of way," she went on hastily. "I mean just noticing things about people—little things that someone else might not notice. It's what I'm used to doing anyway, because of always being new and having to figure things out. And it's good that I don't know any of the other kids very well. That way I won't have any—" She searched for the right word.

"Preconceptions," Ms. Gray supplied. "Well, yes, I see what you mean, Meredith, but—"

"Like in gym tomorrow," Meredith said, "I could notice if anyone from our homeroom is acting different around Ms. Carasso. You know, sneaking looks at her behind her back or acting jumpy or scared or something."

"Or especially pleased with him- or herself," Ms. Gray said grimly. She shook her head. "I doubt it's that simple, Meredith. I'm afraid the person we're looking for may not be at all obvious—not an obvious troublemaker, I mean—and not necessarily someone you'd consider a nerd or a weirdo or a spaz, or whatever the current term is."

She smiled briefly, but went on in a somber voice, "In fact, it may be a person everyone likes, someone we all think of as normal and happy and well adjusted."

Meredith stared at her. "But—but that makes it almost impossible! You mean the person is always *pretending*?"

"Again, not necessarily. Let's just say it's someone who isn't quite what he or she appears to be."

Meredith thought about this. Of course, most people weren't always what they seemed, but usually that had to do with ordinary, everyday things—pretending to get the point of a joke when they really didn't, acting nice to someone they didn't like but needed to stay on the good side of.

She said, "Well, that's another thing I could be watching for. And then after a while, I could make a list of the kids I think would be most likely. Or maybe it'd be easier to start with the ones who're least likely. And then you could check the list and see what you think."

Ms. Gray shook her head. "I don't think we can rule anyone out at this point," she said. "Of course, I have my own ideas about who among your classmates would be capable of composing a poison pen letter and who wouldn't. But beyond that . . ." She hesitated. "It's true that as a teacher I'm at a disadvantage—on the outside looking in, so to speak. Whereas you . . ."

Again she paused, then seemed to come to a decision. "I said I didn't want to involve you further, Meredith, and I'm still not happy about the idea. But since it looks as though I'm not going to be able to stop you anyway, I think perhaps you'd better understand just how vicious this thing is."

She got up and closed the door, then reached for her briefcase. "I can't show you Ms. Carasso's letter, so I'll say only that it referred to small children. But this is the letter Mrs. Norman received."

She handed Meredith a single sheet of paper. It was ordinary typing paper, with cut-out words and letters glued to it above a grainy newspaper photograph that had been neatly trimmed around the edges. The letters were a jumble of different sizes and type styles, but what they said was clear enough:

WOULDN'T DOLORES BE A SMASHING NAME FOR A GIRL BABY?

The photo showed a motorcycle accident on a freeway—a sprawl of twisted metal and broken glass, a pool of something dark and sticky on the pavement. In the background, a figure on a stretcher was being loaded into an ambulance. One leather-jacketed arm hung down limply, as if the person had been badly hurt and was dying—was perhaps already dead.

CHAPTER 8

"Mr. Norman rides a motorcycle," Meredith explained, telling her parents about it that evening. She still felt sick, thinking of Mrs. Norman opening that envelope on the stairway, while her baby turned and kicked inside her. "And the name Dolores . . . that's part of what Ms. Gray meant by internal evidence."

"All those names you looked up for Mrs. Norman," her mother said slowly.

"Yes. It means 'sorrows.' I remember we all wondered why anyone would call a girl Dolores, because of the name being so sad. And 'smashing' comes from something Mrs. Norman read us at the beginning of the year about English slang words—British ones, I mean. Like it's not a word most American kids would think of using."

"And the letter to the gym teacher?"

Meredith shook her head. "I guess it was the same kind of thing. Only the picture would have had something to do with"—she swallowed—"a little girl."

There was a silence in the family room, where Meredith had requested a private conversation after dinner. Ms. Gray had insisted that she tell her parents about the poison pen letters. If Meredith was going to play detective, no matter how quietly and perhaps fruitlessly, it had to be with their knowledge and permission. Meredith didn't mind— she'd felt so upset all day that it was a relief to let her feelings show.

Captain Harding got to his feet and began pacing back and forth in front of the empty fireplace. "Well, I know how I'd handle this business," he said. "I'd interrogate every single kid in that class about the letters until I knew which one of 'em was lying. I'd also take a good look around for things like scissors and glue and old newspapers."

"But everyone has scissors and glue and news-papers," Meredith objected, though in a way it was the same idea that had occurred to her. But as for looking around—

"Matter of fact, we had a case like this back

when I was a midshipman," her father continued, coming to a halt. "Sailor blamed another sailor for stealing his girl, started sending him anonymous letters telling him what was going to happen to him next time he got leave. Nothing to it—the officers conducted a search, and sure enough, they turned up a nasty little stash of clippings and scissors and so on under the sailor's mattress."

He resumed his pacing. Usually that was enough to make Meredith and her mother smile. Even when he was ashore for several months, doing work-ups and test runs and otherwise keeping Monday-to-Friday office hours, Phil Harding always resorted to pacing an imaginary deck when he had a problem to work out.

But neither of them was smiling now.

"Well, I guess you can do stuff like that in the navy—" Meredith began.

"Yes," said her mother. "For heaven's sake, Phil, this is a middle school we're talking about, not the armed services! Interrogations, conducted searches—?" She shook her head, shifting position on the battered brown leather couch that had followed them from base to base. "I can see it's a tricky situation for Ms. Gray, and I suppose for the principal as well."

She looked inquiringly at Meredith, who

shrugged. She hadn't thought about it, but of course Mr. Leonard, the principal, must know about the letters.

"And there's something else." Uncharacteristically, Joyce Harding hesitated. "I can't help worrying that Meredith might wind up being . . . well, at risk in some way." Immediately she looked shamefaced; worries were something she rarely confessed to having. "Not that that's a reason for not trying to help. Still"—she turned again to Meredith, who was sitting on the low hassock next to the TV—"I think you ought to be careful."

"Oh, Mom! At risk from some letters? Anyway, they've got nothing to do with me—it's the teachers who are getting them. Well, teachers and Mrs. Reilly. People who work at the school, or used to."

"All women so far, aren't they?" Captain Harding paused again, frowning out at the patio, where a spray of crimson bougainvillea blazed against the fence in the gathering dusk. "And all women the kids seem to like."

Meredith nodded. That word "seem" again.

He sighed. "Well, I guess I don't see where that gets us. I suppose the letter writer could be a boy who resents women in authority. Or maybe a girl who's jealous of attractive young women in general."

"Except that wouldn't apply in the case of this Mrs. Reilly," Mrs. Harding pointed out. "An older woman, didn't you say, Meredith?"

Meredith nodded again. In the silence, she could hear the thud of a basketball against the backboard over the garage, where Dan was playing a mock game of one-on-one with Peter. Lindsay had kitchen duty tonight, and anyway knew better than to interrupt. It was understood in the Harding family that when you asked for a private briefing, privacy was what you got.

"I started making a list of people I think it could be," Meredith said reluctantly. "Just from things I've noticed so far." She paused, feeling it wasn't right somehow to mention names. "Like there are a couple of kids who really hate school and never do any work if they can help it."

She stopped again, thinking how dumb that sounded. There'd been kids like that at every school she'd ever been to, but that didn't mean they sat down and composed poison pen letters to send to the staff.

"And there are a couple of others who are kind of weird. Like they're fixated on some celebrity, or they think the world's going to be taken over by aliens in the year 2000. Or they're real particular about little things—you know, there's a special pen they always have to write with, and everything in their locker has to be just so."

Meredith wasn't quite sure why she'd brought this up—she was thinking of a mousy girl named Mary Lee Mumford, who was surely too nervous and timid to be the letter writer—but her mother nodded. "People who are obsessive," she said thoughtfully. "Or compulsive, I guess that's a better word. Yes, that might make sense."

Meredith was struck by a new idea—a name that hadn't been on her list. "Do you think someone who'd write stuff on walls—you know, graffiti—might write poison pen letters, too?"

"It could be a logical next step," her father agreed.

"Except that's a public kind of thing," Mrs. Harding objected. "I mean, graffiti is out there for everyone to read and be shocked by—that's the whole point. But this is secret, and meant for just one person. One person at a time, anyway. Also it involves a lot more planning and effort than just sneaking around with a spray can." She bit her lip. "Oh, dear, it's unpleasant to think about, isn't it?"

"Yes." Meredith stood up abruptly. "I guess I don't want to talk about this anymore right now, okay? I think I'll go see if Lindsay wants to play backgammon." She and Lindsay had a running game whose score now totaled in the tens of thousands. Meredith was 600 points behind but catching up.

"Only if she's finished in the kitchen," her mother said firmly, and followed Meredith out of the room to check. Lindsay had; the kitchen was immaculate, except for a wet dishrag slung over the gleaming faucet. Lindsay always managed to forget some one thing.

Mrs. Harding sighed. "I'm sorry Ms. Gray had to involve you in this business, Meredith," she said as she wrung out the dishrag and stowed it on its rack beneath the sink. "It's hard enough being new, I know, without feeling you have to keep watch over your classmates in this creepy way."

"I involved myself," Meredith corrected her unhappily. "If I hadn't looked out the window when I did . . . and I didn't *have* to say anything to Ms. Gray. But anyway, it's better that I'm new. Like I don't have a whole lot at stake," she explained, having thought about this since that morning. "Not like the other kids do, that've known each other since kindergarten and everything. The ones who really live here, I mean."

"Not having a lot at stake," her mother said slowly. "Is that how you feel?"

Meredith shrugged. "Well, sort of. But it's okay. I mean, I'm used to it, and I'm not complaining or anything." But she found herself looking at her mother with sudden hope. "Do you think we might ever get to go back somewhere?"

"Go back?"

"Like to Washington State? Or even Georgia?" It had been very hot in Georgia.

Mrs. Harding looked puzzled. "I thought you liked it here."

"I do. I just meant . . . well, next time we move, it'd be nice if we could go back to someplace we've lived before. You know, where I'd already know some of the kids and the fun things to do and what to wear and stuff like that."

"I don't honestly think there's much chance of that, Meredith. Not with the kind of work your father does."

Mrs. Harding seemed about to add something more, but checked herself. She gave Meredith's shoulders a quick squeeze and said, "One thing we can do, though, is plan some fun things for you to do with your new friends here. Peter's happy with his pals in the neighborhood, but you're at the age where I know just hanging around the house isn't very exciting."

Her eyes had brightened. Meredith recognized the look—one thing her mother loved was making plans.

"Yes," Mrs. Harding went on, "why don't you invite someone for this Saturday? Your father and I have a golf date, but Dan could take you wherever you wanted to go. The beach or Horton Plaza or Balboa Park—I hear the space museum there is a lot of fun. We'll give you an advance on your allowance, or maybe even a raise. I think you're about due for one."

Meredith was pleased, but said doubtfully, "Dan wouldn't want to do that. Anyway, doesn't he have to work on Saturday?" Dan had gotten a part-time job at McDonald's to start earning money for a new car.

"Dan will do what I ask him to do," her mother assured her crisply. "And he doesn't have to be at work until five. Now, who will it be—Corky, or Emily, or that nice Connie Morales we met at the library the other day?"

Meredith considered. "I don't have to decide right now, do I?"

"No, but you probably ought to get it set up by tomorrow night so I can tell Dan and put it on the schedule. I'll need Lindsay here to baby-sit Peter, so I don't want her taking a sitting job somewhere else. Or making plans with Fred."

Fred was the boy Lindsay had gone out with. She was still waiting for him to call again—probably sitting in her room right now with the door open so she could get to the phone first if it rang.

As Meredith went upstairs, she ran over Saturday's choices in her mind. She owed Corky—not that Corky thought of it that way, she was sure—but Corky would probably want to spend the whole day at Horton Plaza, and although it was one of the neatest malls Meredith had ever seen, malls weren't really her thing. Emily, she knew, usually had to work at her parents' garden center on weekends. As for Connie Morales . . .

Meredith hated having to think in this new, suspicious way, but the fact was that Connie's name was on the list she'd made that afternoon.

She was almost positive that Connie was too gentle and sweet-natured to think ill of anyone, let alone send them a vicious poison pen letter. Still, she'd found herself remembering something she'd overheard Connie say to Tina Vallejo on the first day of school. Meredith couldn't recall Connie's exact words, but the gist was that she'd heard Mrs. Norman tended not to expect too much of Latino kids.

Connie had said this without rancor, as if simply stating a fact—and later Meredith had thought uncomfortably that it might be true, from the way Mrs. Norman smiled a lot at Tina and Connie and the others but hardly ever called on them in class. But what if something more had happened, some hurtful incident Meredith didn't know about, that showed Mrs. Norman really was prejudiced? Could that have upset Connie to the point where she'd want to hurt Mrs. Norman back?

Meredith pushed the idea away. Virginia Robb, she thought suddenly. Yes, Virginia would be the perfect person to invite for Saturday. It would be a way of getting to know her better, as Ms. Gray had seemed to suggest she should.

Meredith tried not to let herself think that Virginia was also a safe choice because of being new—someone she wouldn't have to watch and wonder about the whole time she was with her.

CHAPTER 9

The hardest part about the oral history project had turned out to be finding long-time residents to interview. Many of the older people in San Diego were recent arrivals in the area—retirees attracted by the climate and by the varied facilities for senior citizens.

Nor did it help Meredith's team that Sara Freeman and Deirdre Loomis were in charge of making the initial phone calls, using names compiled from voting lists and real estate records.

Sara made no secret of the fact that she considered the whole project boring and stupid. "Who wants to hang out with a bunch of old geezers with hearing aids and bad breath?" she'd complained.

As for Deirdre, a spacey girl with vague blue eyes and a mass of pale-blond hair, she had such a faint, breathy voice that she'd probably be inaudible over the phone to anyone with even a minor hearing problem. Corky thought Deirdre might be doing drugs. "It's not a big problem here at La Playa," Corky said. "Still, if you know who's dealing—" She'd shrugged.

In addition to Jeff Barlow and Noah Wright, the remaining members of their team were a quiet African-American boy named David Howe and skinny, monkey-faced Pete Sanchez, the class clown. David wasn't on Meredith's list of suspects, but Pete was, along with Deirdre and Noah.

Ms. Gray had shaken her head at these names. "I know I told you not to rule anyone out, Meredith—but Noah? I've known Noah since he was in kindergarten. He may be hyperactive and a bit foolish at times, but I'd swear there isn't a mean bone in his body. As for Deirdre, it seems to take all her energy and concentration just to put her earrings on in the morning."

Meredith grinned at that but said, "I know, but you can never tell what she's going to do next. If she got into some kind of weird mood. . . ." She stopped, not wanting to mention the possibility that Deirdre might be using drugs.

"Unpredictable," Ms. Gray said, and sighed. "Well, yes, I suppose there is that. Pete Sanchez, though—" She broke off to close the nearest window, even though there was no one in sight outside. They were meeting after school, supposedly to go over some extra work she was giving Meredith in math. "Why on earth would you suspect Pete?"

"Well, he's always kidding around—you know, making wisecracks and doing imitations of people and asking these corny riddles he gets out of some old joke book. I just thought if he got carried away, he might think it was funny to make up a poison pen letter. He might be sorry he sent it, but by then it would be too late."

Ms. Gray shook her head even more decisively than before. "Pete knows the difference between a funny practical joke and a cruel one." She sat back, regarding Meredith with a troubled expression. "Oh, dear, I hate to see you turning everyone inside out this way, Meredith. I'm afraid I didn't realize how confusing this was going to be for you."

Ms. Gray hesitated. "I notice you've been spending a good deal of time with Virginia Robb lately. I hope it's not just because she's new, too, and therefore above suspicion." She smiled, but her blue eyes were serious.

Meredith shook her head, though it was true

that might have been part of it to begin with.

"I really have fun with Virginia," she said. She told Ms. Gray about the Saturday they'd spent together. At Virginia's suggestion, they'd loaded their bikes into the station wagon and had Dan drop them off at the beginning of the Point Loma peninsula. They'd cycled all the way out to the Cabrillo National Monument at the end, then climbed down the cliffs to explore the tide pools on the ocean side of the point.

"I'm not usually too good about things like crabs and jellyfish and octopuses," Meredith confessed. "You know, things that have too many legs or move in a weird way. But Virginia's never lived near the ocean before, and she was really excited about all the stuff we saw. Besides, it's beautiful there."

"One of my own favorite spots," Ms. Gray told her with a smile. She added, "And one of the nicest things about new friends, I think, is learning to see things through their eyes, in a whole new way."

She looked at her watch, sighed, and slid a stack of test papers into her briefcase. "Well, you'd better run along now, Meredith. I'm sorry to have made you miss your bus."

Meredith explained that she'd ridden her bike and that, anyway, she was in no hurry to get home. Lindsay had finally heard from Fred and had invited him over for dinner that night. She planned to spend the afternoon making her special spaghetti sauce. Lindsay in the kitchen with a lot of canned tomatoes was a scene Meredith would just as soon miss.

What she did mind was sneaking around this way, though she didn't say so. She had a feeling Ms. Gray didn't enjoy it any more than she did.

As the weeks went by, though, there were no more poison pen letters, and Meredith thought maybe Ms. Gray had been right about the writer's wanting publicity. He or she must have been disappointed when there was no mention of the letter Ms. Carasso had received.

Gradually, Meredith let herself relax. Instead of looking for hidden meanings in things people said and did, she found herself reacting normally again—laughing at Pete, getting disgusted with Sara, trading library books with Connie Morales (who loved to read as much as Meredith did), despairing over Noah Wright and his nonstop mouth.

Actually, Noah was turning out to be an unexpectedly useful member of their oral history team. At first they'd been afraid the person they were interviewing would never be able to get a word in edgewise. Then they realized that Noah's chatter tended to relax the person—either that or make him mad.

"Now hold on a minute, sonny," one old man had said, raising a leathery hand. "I expect what you had for breakfast this morning ain't nearly as interesting as what I had for breakfast back in '37—or was it '38?—anyway, the year I was mate on a tuna boat that went aground in a storm off Baja. . . ."

Although the teams were supposed to limit their research to residents of the neighborhoods they'd been assigned, Ms. Gray had said that if they heard of someone really special in another part of the city, she'd try to arrange transportation.

"When I did this project with another class years ago, there were plenty of mothers available to drive," she'd told them ruefully. "Now, of course, they're all at work during the day."

Sara Freeman had stared at Ms. Gray, then closed her social studies book with a clap that woke up Adam Kowalski, dozing as usual at the back of the room. "You mean this whole thing's been *done* before?" she demanded. "Then why do we have to do it all over again?"

"To learn something, Sara," Ms. Gray had said with a sigh. "Possibly even to learn something about good manners."

During a team conference in early November, Jeff Barlow told them about someone his mother had met, a widow who lived in La Jolla and who was a third-generation San Diegan. She herself wasn't all that old—in her sixties, he thought—but she remembered a lot of stories her parents and grandparents had told her, and she'd said she'd be happy to talk to the group. She also had some old photographs she could let them copy for their scrapbook.

"Oh, wow, La Jolla," Deirdre said, widening her blue eyes at Jeff. "Your mom must travel in the fast lane, right?" La Jolla—"La Hoya," as Meredith had learned to pronounce it—was a wealthy community on the shore north of Pacific Beach.

Meredith didn't think Deirdre was being sarcastic (though it was sometimes hard to tell with her), but she saw Jeff's ears redden. His parents had been divorced soon after the move from Michigan, and it was clear from his lack of spending money that he and his mother and older sister sometimes had a hard time making ends meet.

"My mother's a nurse," he said shortly. "That's how she got to know Mrs. Craig—she broke her leg and wound up at Scripps Clinic, where my mom works."

"Not everyone in La Jolla is rich," Ms. Gray

observed mildly. "I live there myself. As a matter of fact, I know Alice Craig slightly, and I think she'd be an excellent person to talk to. I'll see what I can arrange."

Corky said, "Well, let's hope she has some really good stuff to tell us. I mean, Emily's team found that guy who worked on Lindbergh's plane, and we don't have anyone like that." *The Spirit of St. Louis,* she meant, which had been built in San Diego.

"This isn't a competition, Corky," Ms. Gray reminded her.

"I know, but wouldn't it be neat if we turned up a real celebrity? Like maybe they were famous once, but now they're forgotten and living in—in obscurity."

Corky's eyes were sparkling; even Ms. Gray smiled as she shook her head at her.

"Yeah!" Noah exclaimed. "They could've changed their name, even. Hey, what *about* that? Like some old-time movie star might be living right around here, and we wouldn't even know it."

He ransacked his memory, which Meredith pictured as being a little like Dagwood's closet—you never knew what might tumble out when you opened the door. "That little guy with the funny walk, for instance, what's-his-name, Charlie

Chaplin. Or I know, Douglas Fairbanks! Not Douglas Fairbanks, Jr., but the first one—he even had a house around here somewhere. Well, I guess he's supposed to be dead, but it could be like Elvis . . ."

"Oh, Noah," everyone groaned.

CHAPTER

10

Mrs. Craig lived in the maze of winding, hilly roads above the glossy shopping streets of La Jolla. Mr. Ramirez, the art teacher, who was driving the group in his van, had to stop to consult his map several times before they pulled up at last in front of a small, square cottage with a green-painted front door and a scalloped roof of dark old Spanish tiles.

Luckily it was a warm, sunny morning, so they were able to interview Mrs. Craig in her backyard. They would never have all squeezed into the tiny living room.

"As a matter of fact, there's a good deal of local history right here," Mrs. Craig observed, leaning on her crutch to wave a hand at the colorful flower beds surrounding her patio. She was a small, spare woman with bright hazel eyes behind gold-rimmed glasses. Her vigorous manner belied the heavy cast she still wore on one leg.

"San Diego has very little in the way of native vegetation," she explained. "Almost all of the plants and shrubs and trees you see blooming in people's gardens and in public places come from somewhere else."

"Right," Noah said importantly. "Without all the water that's piped in, we'd be living in a desert, practically."

"Well, *chaparral*, anyway," Mrs. Craig agreed, as she put out a hand to stop a stack of paper cups from blowing off the patio table, where she'd set out a pitcher of juice and a plate of cookies. "Though we're certainly getting a desert wind today." She grimaced. "Good tourist weather, I know, and I ought to be used to it by now, but the Santa Ana always makes me feel peculiar—wired, I think you kids would say."

Meredith realized that the breeze was coming from the east instead of from the west, the way it usually did. That must be why the air was so clear today, every outline so sharp and bright that it almost hurt your eyes to focus on anything for more than a few seconds. The ocean glittering beyond the rooftops and clustered palm trees was a deep, hard blue.

"Anyway," Mrs. Craig went on, "a lot of the plants you see here in my garden came from Hawaii originally, and many others from South America. In fact, this is really their third home, since I grew many of them from cuttings taken from my grandfather's garden in Mission Hills. He was a sea captain, like his father before him," she explained, "until he turned to shipbuilding. My great-great-grandfather was a whaler, I'm sorry to say. His home port was New Bedford, Massachusetts, but he resettled here in the eighteen-sixties, when San Diego was still just an adobe village on a hill. . . ."

While she talked, Meredith made notes about the house and garden and about Mrs. Craig herself for David to use later when he transcribed Noah's tape—David was what Ms. Gray called their scribe. Jeff and Pete were responsible for asking the questions. Mrs. Craig talked so easily, though, settling into a wicker lounge chair and propping her cast on a cushion, that they soon put away their lists and sprawled on the grass to listen.

Even Sara and Deirdre looked less bored than usual, although Sara's face never quite lost its scowl—maybe she'd been born with it, Meredith thought—and it was hard to tell what Deirdre was actually seeing when she stared fixedly at someone with her large light-blue eyes.

Only Corky seemed restless, playing with the strap of her camera while her gaze roved from the ocean view to the set of wind chimes rattling musically beneath the cottage eaves. Meredith had to give her a nudge to remind her to take pictures of the special plants Mrs. Craig mentioned, also of the small bronze statue of an Indian boy with a fishing net that her grandfather had commissioned for the Panama Exposition in Balboa Park in 1916.

"Are you feeling okay?" Meredith asked when the hour was up and they were filing back along the flagstone path that ran beside the cottage.

Corky shrugged, ducking under a blossom-laden hibiscus bush. "I don't like Santa Anas, either. They give me a headache, sort of, like my brains are drying up inside my head."

Meredith had been enjoying the summery November heat, but it was true that the air felt unnaturally dry against her skin, her mouth especially. She wished she'd brought some Chapstick along.

"What a neat lady," Jeff said as they took their places in the van, then looked embarrassed— enthusiasm wasn't his usual style. "I mean, all those stories her grandfather told her about when the railroad was being built, and the political stuff, too . . . that's gonna be great for our report."

"Yeah," Noah said, his eyes shining. "And what about that party she had when she was eighteen? Like her parents rented out the whole Hotel Del Coronado, and invited all those celebrities and movie stars and everything."

"Right, you even got your Douglas Fairbanks," Pete teased him, flourishing an imaginary sword in the air. "I wonder what happened to her money," he added, sliding hastily into his seat as the van started off. "Maybe they blew it all on the party. You wouldn't think she'd end up living in a dinky little place like that."

"I thought it was nice," Meredith protested. "I wouldn't mind living in a house like that when I get old."

"Well, sure, but you're not used to having a butler and a maid and a bathroom as big as the whole living room she has now, probably. I mean, have you ever seen some of those places up around Presidio Park where she grew up? My dad put in a terrace for some rich guy there a while back, and man, talk about having room to spread out." Pete's father was a stonemason.

Deirdre said suddenly, "I just now realized who that lady reminded me of." Pete rolled his eyes; as usual, Deirdre was off on her own mental track. "Mrs. Reilly. Yeah, that's who, exactly."

"Oh, come on," Jeff said, laughing. "Mrs. Reilly?"

"Well, they're both little and skinny and sort of quick," Deirdre insisted. "And they both wear glasses."

"Deirdre, lots of people wear glasses," Sara told her impatiently, while the others groaned and shook their heads. Meredith felt uneasy somehow at the mention of Mrs. Reilly's name, and wondered if anyone else did.

Noah said, "It's too bad she has to have that big cast on her leg, though—Mrs. Craig, I mean. I had to have a cast once, when I broke my arm playing dodgeball, remember? And it itched like crazy, way down inside. Oh, hey, you guys, we should've asked Mrs. Craig if we could write on her cast! You know, have everyone sign their name—like it'd be a way of saying thank you. Yeah, maybe we still could. Mr. Ramirez, you think you could turn around? We forgot something."

He leaned forward to tap the art teacher on the shoulder. Mr. Ramirez just scowled and shook his head. The van was already in bumper-to-bumper traffic on Torrey Pines Road.

"Easy, man," said David, pulling Noah back down beside him. "She'll probably be getting the cast off soon anyway."

Jeff said with a frown, "Well, I hope so, but my

mom said it was a really bad break. Sometimes older people take a long time to heal. And that's not so good because meanwhile all the muscles stop working, and if it takes too long, they can—" He paused, searching for the word.

"Atrophy," Corky supplied, with one of her surprising bursts of word power. She'd been uncharacteristically quiet, and Meredith thought her head must really be hurting.

"Yeah, and if that happened, Mrs. Craig might never walk right again, or at least not without a bad limp."

Even Noah was silent while they all considered this.

Then Sara gave one of her loud guffaws. "Hey, did you hear how she broke it? She was skin diving off La Jolla Cove on a rough day, and a big wave came along and smashed her against a rock. An old biddy like that—I think that's a crock. I mean, can you see Mrs. Craig in a wetsuit?"

Meredith sighed, deciding Sara was one of those people you had to work hard at liking for more than about five minutes at a time.

It was only when the van was turning into the school parking lot that they realized they'd never collected the photo albums Mrs. Craig had said they could borrow.

"Darn," said Jeff. "And she had them out for us, too, on that table in the living room. Corky, you should have remembered—you're supposed to be in charge of pictures."

"Sorry, sorry!" Corky said crossly, making a fending-off motion with her hands. "Anyway, no big loss. They'd probably be mostly pictures of her dear little grandchildren, the way she kept talking about them."

Meredith frowned. She didn't remember Mrs. Craig talking about her grandchildren, except to mention that two of them lived in England and she sent them oranges and figs from her fruit trees every Christmas. Corky was just in a bad mood because of the Santa Ana, she decided—and maybe also because Mr. Ramirez hadn't been paying her any special attention. Corky liked to think she was his star pupil, but as far as Meredith could see, he treated her just as impatiently as he did everyone else.

The Santa Ana wind continued to blow all that week, sending inland temperatures into the nineties under a cloudless, cobalt-blue sky that looked as if it had been enameled. Sometimes there was grit in the wind that got into your eyes and nostrils. If you were in a carpeted room, you had to watch out for nasty little electric shocks when you touched anything metal.

Still, Meredith thought of the bitter wind that would be blowing off Narragansett Bay right about now, stripping the remaining leaves from the trees and rattling windowpanes, while furnaces kicked on and parents shook their heads over the oil bill. Here in the sunshine, it was hard to believe Thanksgiving was only two weeks away.

As the week went on, there were brushfires throughout the county—fire was always a danger during hot, dry Santa Ana weather. Human tempers flared, too. Meredith didn't have the wired feeling Mrs. Craig had described, but she could see that the weather made some people jumpy and irritable. Lindsay broke up and reunited with Fred twice in the course of three days. Dan carried on an interminable argument with his father about the car he wanted to buy, a twelve-year-old Mazda he'd heard about from a friend. Captain Harding said he should buy American; Dan said the only American cars he could afford would cost him more in gas than he was spending now on bus fare to get to his job.

All in all, it was a relief when the weather broke over the weekend, giving way to clouds and a gentle, moist west wind.

CHAPTER 11

"Mrs. *Craig?*"

Meredith stared in disbelief from Ms. Gray to Mr. Leonard, the school principal. They were in Mr. Leonard's office, where Meredith had been summoned at lunchtime on Monday.

"But that's terrible! She's such a nice lady. Why would anyone . . . who would ever . . . ?" She was stammering so badly she could hardly get the words out.

"We're hoping you'll have some ideas about that, Meredith," Mr. Leonard said, waving her to a chair beside his cluttered desk. He was a large, untidy man with shrewd brown eyes under shaggy salt-and-pepper eyebrows. The kids called him Leo because of the way he sometimes prowled the halls, casual but alert. If you weren't where you were supposed to be, you made sure you got there quickly.

He turned to Ms. Gray, who stood by the window—the closed window, Meredith noticed—with her arms folded tightly across her chest and her face grimmer than Meredith had ever seen it.

"One thing I don't understand, Katherine," he said. "Why did this Mrs. Craig think of calling you? I mean, why would she immediately assume it was one of the kids who sent the letter?"

"That's something Meredith can tell you, I'm afraid."

Ms. Gray nodded at the single sheet of typing paper in front of him. With a sigh, he turned it around and pushed it across the desk where Meredith could see it.

This time the photograph was on glossy paper, obviously cut from a magazine. It showed an ancient bag lady sitting on a grimy stoop, wrapped in layers of old sweaters and scarves. She was holding a child's battered plastic pinwheel in one clawlike hand and grinning toothlessly at the camera. But the really horrifying thing about the picture was the fact that the bag lady had only one leg.

IT TAKES TWO LEGS TO TANGO was the message beneath the picture.

Angry tears stung Meredith's eyes, blurring the patchwork letters.

She said, "The party at the fancy hotel when she was eighteen. Mrs. Craig said she did the tango with some old-time movie star. I can't remember his name, except he was Spanish or South American or something, with that black, slicked-back hair they used to have." She swallowed. "He had a flower in his buttonhole that got smashed when she didn't change direction in time, and the petals all turned brown and fell off. It was really funny, the way she told it."

Ms. Gray nodded. "A gardenia." She looked at the principal. "Alice Craig says it's been years since she mentioned her debutante party to anyone, let alone told that particular story. She put two and two together and called me."

She turned back to Meredith. "Again, we've had the letter and envelope checked for fingerprints, and again, except for some post office smudges, the only clear prints are Mrs. Craig's and those of a friend who happened to be with her when she opened it. Luckily, I'd say." She shook her head. "She tried to make light of it on the phone, but when I went to see her yesterday, I could see it had been a dreadful shock."

"I'd think so." Mr. Leonard grunted. "Imagine being nice enough to invite a group of kids into your home and then being rewarded with something like *this*."

He pulled the letter toward him again, stared at it for a moment, and then turned it facedown on the desk.

Ms. Gray said to Meredith, "You realize this narrows things down considerably."

Meredith nodded miserably. "It's someone on our team." She shook her head. "It's hard to believe. I know I put some of their names on my list, but I never really thought it could be one of them. And to pick on Mrs. Craig—"

She broke off, thinking of the peaceful, sunny hour in the garden, trying to imagine someone going home and searching through a pile of magazines and newspapers for a picture and words that would hurt and sting like the sudden, unexpected lash of a scorpion's tail. "It's—it's *evil*," she said.

"Evil." Ms. Gray seemed to ponder the word. "Maybe. Sick, certainly."

In the silence, Meredith could hear the shouts and laughter of kids milling around outside during the noontime break. She'd brought lunch to school today and had been finishing her apple at one of the outdoor tables when another student came up to her with the message that Ms. Gray wanted to see her. The kid hadn't said where until they got inside. "Wow, Ms. Gray and Mr. Leonard both!" she'd whispered, wide-eyed. "What'd you *do*?"

Mr. Leonard said thoughtfully, leaning back in his chair, "Sick, but also asking for help, wouldn't you say?" When Ms. Gray looked at him inquiringly, he explained, "Well, as you both said, this narrows the possibilities to what—eight people?"

"Seven, if you don't count me," Meredith said, not smiling; she felt as if she might never smile again.

"And of course the culprit must realize that. From what you say, he or she worded the message in such a way that Mrs. Craig would almost certainly connect it with the research team and report it to the school."

"Like the letter sent to Carol Norman," Ms. Gray said slowly, "tying it to someone in her homeroom. At the time, I thought of that as a kind of dare—'catch me if you can'—but perhaps it was more than that." She was silent, thinking. "After which the writer panicked or changed his mind—his or her mind—and sent a letter to Ms. Carasso that could have come from anyone."

Meredith blurted, "But why send them at all? That's what I don't understand."

"I think maybe it's something the person has to

do, Meredith," Ms. Gray said somberly. "Perhaps without really wanting to, or understanding why." She looked at Mr. Leonard. "Yes, I think you're right. In a way, this latest letter is a cry for help."

"Why can't the person just *ask* for help, then?" Meredith asked, feeling troubled and confused. She'd been hating the letter writer, but maybe that was wrong of her. Maybe she should be feeling sorry for the person instead, no matter how much pain the letters had caused.

Ms. Gray shook her head. "I don't know," she said. "If we knew that, I think we'd also know who it is."

After a pause, Mr. Leonard cleared his throat and said, "I know this is tough on you, Meredith— but I'd like you to spend some time thinking about the morning you spent with Mrs. Craig. Did anything happen that could have upset someone? Did anyone behave oddly, or seem hostile toward Mrs. Craig? Even if it's just a little thing, something that didn't strike you as important at the time, make a note of it and let Ms. Gray know. Okay?"

Meredith nodded uncertainly. A little thing? But someone must have been terribly angry at Mrs. Craig in order to have sent that cruel letter. How could she have missed something like that?

"Meanwhile, I think you should talk to Dr. Egan again," Mr. Leonard told Ms. Gray. Dr. Egan was the school psychologist. "I know you've consulted him before, but now that we have a much shorter list . . ." He shrugged. "Well, maybe he'll be able to see something we've missed."

As he pushed back his chair, Ms. Gray said slowly, "You know, I have a feeling something more may happen soon—that this child may be approaching some kind of breaking point."

Mr. Leonard glanced at Meredith and seemed to hesitate. Then, as if deciding she could be trusted with what he was about to say, he nodded and said, "Yes. And probably the best thing that could happen, provided help is close at hand."

"Something more?" Meredith said, looking from one to the other. "Another letter, you mean?"

Ms. Gray said, "Possibly. But possibly something more . . . direct." It was her turn to hesitate. "If you notice someone behaving strangely, Meredith—not responding appropriately, say, or losing control for no apparent reason—I want you to promise you'll tell me or another adult at once."

"Well, sure," Meredith said blankly. It was what she'd been looking for all along, after all—someone behaving strangely. Losing control, though . . . what exactly did Ms. Gray mean by that?

In the doorway, Mr. Leonard gave Meredith's arm a quick squeeze. "I'm sorry we've had to put you through this, Meredith. But I think Ms. Gray is right—it may be almost over. If you remember something that might help, let us know. Meanwhile, try not to worry too much, okay?" The brown eyes beneath the shaggy brows were kindly and concerned.

Ms. Gray said, practically, "I don't think your research team has any interviews scheduled for this week, does it?" Meredith shook her head, relieved to realize that this was true. "And next week it'll be time for the Thanksgiving break. Heavens, how time flies!"

"You mean you're not ready for a vacation, Katherine?" Mr. Leonard teased as he ushered them into the outer office. "Now that's what I like to hear from my staff."

"I didn't say I wasn't counting the days," Ms. Gray retorted.

Meredith went slowly back outside through the main doors. It was almost time for the bell to ring, but somehow she needed to be out under the sky again, never mind the clouds and the chilly breeze. Also she'd left her sweater on the bench where she'd eaten lunch with her friends.

As Meredith rounded the corner of the building,

she saw that everyone had left the table except Corky. Her steps slowed; she didn't feel like talking to anyone right now, not even Corky. But it was too late—Corky had spotted her and was waving Meredith's red cardigan in the air like a flag.

"I've just had the neatest idea," she said as Meredith approached. "You know those two black kittens the Lesters have been trying to give away?" Meredith nodded. The Lesters were neighbors of Corky's, with the biggest house on the block and a manicured lawn they were always watering. "Well, I've been bugging Paula to let me take them, and finally she said I could have one, but not both."

"That's great," Meredith said mechanically. She added, "I mean, one kitten is better than nothing." She knew how much Corky wanted a pet, preferably a dog. But Paula had said firmly that they weren't getting a dog until Will was at least three or four and could be taught how to treat one.

"Yeah, but it's a real shame to separate them," Corky said. "I mean, they look exactly alike, and also they have so much fun together I swear, they play regular games like tag and hide-and-seek in those big bushes in the Lesters' side yard. So what I thought was"—she beamed at Meredith—"you could take one kitten and I could take the other. Then we could bring them over to each other's houses to play, and they'd hardly be separated at all."

Meredith sighed inwardly. She wasn't in the mood for this. She shook her head. "I told you, Corky, we're through having cats. They're too much trouble when we move. Besides, if we did take one and then we moved, they wouldn't be together anyway."

"Well, maybe you won't," Corky said, as the bell sounded inside the building. "Move, I mean. And even if you did, I bet you wouldn't have any trouble with Inky or Slinky. My names for them," she said with a grin, "but you could change yours. I mean, these are real smart kittens, even if they aren't purebred whatcha-ma-call-its, Himalayans, like their mother. Heaven only knows *who* the father was," she said, imitating Mrs. Lester's prissy manner so perfectly that Meredith smiled in spite of herself. "Oh, come on, Merry, at least say you'll think about it."

Meredith just shook her head again. If only Corky could remember not to call her Merry, she thought for the hundredth time. As for not moving . . . she shivered and pulled the red sweater around her shoulders as she headed for the side door. Right now she wished she'd never even heard of La Playa Middle School. In fact, right now she wouldn't have minded learning they were moving to Antarctica in the morning.

CHAPTER 12

Meredith set her flute aside with a sigh. She'd been playing scales and simple exercises in an effort to distract herself, but it wasn't working.

Mr. Leonard had said not to worry. But how could she not worry, when it looked like this sick, angry person was someone she'd spent a lot time with—someone she'd gotten to know and like? Alone in her room that afternoon, Meredith realized she'd been hoping the poison pen writer would turn out to be someone she barely knew, like Ron Selby or Tim McDermott or even Mary Lee Mumford. But now that didn't seem possible.

Well, she knew and liked everyone except for Sara Freeman and Deirdre Loomis. Not that she disliked Deirdre, exactly—it was hard to dislike someone who didn't seem to be quite *there* a lot of the time. By the same token, though, it was hard to feel you'd ever be able to understand her or trust her.

But maybe it really could be Sara, Meredith thought, flopping down on her bed and staring up at the ceiling.

Sara seemed to have a grudge against almost everyone, and she certainly didn't mind hurting people's feelings. She was always reading magazines, too—cheap horror magazines that she kept hidden between the pages of her math workbook. She definitely had at least one computer at home, since her father was some kind of high-tech business consultant. Meredith had heard Sara bragging about how much he charged per hour, and how they had a vacation house in Hawaii and her mother got to buy a new fur coat every other year. (A fur coat in San Diego? When would she ever wear it?)

Meredith shook her head at herself, knowing she wasn't being fair. No matter how much she wanted the poison pen writer to be Sara, the truth was that everyone in the group probably had both the means and the opportunity, like they said on detective shows.

No, the thing to do was concentrate on the reason for the letters—the motive. And since it was hard to keep all four victims in her head at once, she should focus on the latest one, Mrs. Craig, as Mr. Leonard had suggested. She should also consider each member of the research team in turn, not leaving anyone out and not dismissing any of the reasons she came up with, never mind how weak or farfetched they seemed.

Jeff, for instance, could resent the fact that his mother worked long hours as a nurse and had to take care of women like Mrs. Craig—women who'd had it easy, or who at least had never had to earn their own livings. Corky could think that Mrs. Craig was snobbish because of her family background. Being so open and friendly herself, Corky was critical of anyone she thought was putting on airs. Meredith didn't think Mrs. Craig was really like that, but then, Corky had been in a bad mood that day.

Meredith sighed and went on to Noah. He'd seemed sort of fixated on Mrs. Craig's broken leg, she thought, remembering how he'd wanted Mr. Ramirez to turn the van around so they could go back and write their names on the cast. Maybe he had some weird thing about people who were hurt or injured. Certainly if Noah himself ever had so much as a hangnail or a nosebleed, everyone got to hear about it in boring detail.

Then there was David Howe. Well, David was African-American, and although he wasn't poor or anything—he had a glamorous mother who was a TV anchorwoman—he might hate a person whose family had been part of the white establishment for so many years. Meredith herself had never seen any signs of racism in David, but he was so quiet and self-contained that it was hard to tell what he might be thinking or feeling underneath.

Pete Sanchez was just the opposite, or so Meredith had always thought—everything near the surface, spilling over into jokes and wisecracks. Yet Pete was Mexican, so he too might have reason to hate white people—Anglos—if only because of the immigration laws. Pete made no secret of the fact that his parents had entered the country illegally when he was just a baby, hiding out with relatives in the Los Angeles barrio until his father was able to get a work card and find steady employment as a stonemason.

With six kids, though, the Sanchezes still couldn't be very well off. Meredith thought of what Pete had said about the mansions in Mission Hills. She wouldn't blame him for resenting the kind of luxury Mrs. Craig had probably taken for granted for much of her life.

And now for Deirdre. Meredith bit her lip. If she was honest with herself, she had to agree with Ms. Gray that it was almost impossible to imagine Deirdre's having the patience and concentration to put together the kind of letter Mrs. Craig and the others had received.

On the other hand, there was the strange, intent way Deirdre had sat staring at Mrs. Craig that day—and also the connection she'd made afterward with Mrs. Reilly. Why should Mrs. Reilly have been on Deirdre's mind?

Meredith thought how Deirdre never seemed to eat anything except junk food—and not even real food, just stuff like taco chips and Twinkies and candy bars. If Mrs. Reilly was so big on nutrition, she might have given Deirdre a hard time about her eating habits when she worked at the school cafeteria. She might have embarrassed or humiliated Deirdre in front of other kids, to the point where she'd started hating Mrs. Reilly and made up her mind to get back at her somehow.

And of course if Mrs. Reilly had known or guessed that Deirdre was doing drugs and had said something to her about it, threatened to tell her parents or the school authorities . . . Sure, the whole thing could have started right there.

But Meredith didn't know about the drugs for sure, she reminded herself sharply. Nor did she really know anything about Mrs. Reilly. As for Mrs. Norman and Ms. Carasso . . . did Deirdre even have gym with Ms. Carasso this semester? Meredith didn't think so. Of course she didn't know about last year.

No, this was dumb. In fact, she was acting just like the traditional dumb cop in mystery stories, the one who always wants to arrest the wrong person, never mind whether he has any real facts to go on. Meredith scowled and rolled over, picking at a loose thread in her bedspread—the same boring beige bedspread she'd been stuck with for years because it went with everything. She needed to stick to her original plan, she told herself, and that meant concentrating on Mrs. Craig and how the other kids had reacted to her.

Which brought her back to the remaining member of the team—Sara Freeman.

Sara thought old people were ugly and boring and disgusting. She'd jeered at the idea of Mrs. Craig's going skin diving, just as she'd jeered at a nice old guy they'd met earlier who worked out regularly with weights and entered every 10K race that came along. Probably Sara thought everyone over the age of fifty-five should be euthanized, or at least locked away somewhere. And the next best thing might be hurting them in some cruel, sneaky way, a way they couldn't even fight back against.

Yes, Sara was still her best suspect, Meredith decided . . . until she remembered that two of the four people who'd received the anonymous letters hadn't been old at all, but young, attractive, active women.

❧ ❧ ❧

"Oh, not the Pfeiffers," Lindsay groaned. "Do we have to?"

"Yeah," said Peter, pushing his peas under his potato skin. "They're so old and boring."

Meredith said, "Couldn't we just stay home, and maybe invite some foreign students for Thanksgiving, like we did that time in Georgia?"

Until now, she hadn't given much thought to Thanksgiving Day itself. She and Corky were going to the zoo the day after, and over the weekend she'd planned a hike with Virginia through Torrey Pines State Park, where there were some high bluffs from which they might be lucky enough to see a migrating whale.

Captain Harding looked around the dinner table in some exasperation. "Too bad Dan's at work," he said. "Unless one of you wants to cast a negative vote for him, too?" He raised an eyebrow; no one said anything.

"Now, listen, kids, Admiral Pfeiffer was darned good to me when I was still wet behind the ears. I can't tell you how many times he picked me up and dried me off"—Peter giggled at this—"and if he and his wife are crazy enough to want this whole gang for Thanksgiving dinner, we're going to be there with bells on."

"And it's not a voting matter," said their mother, frowning at Peter, who was having a renewed fit of giggles at the idea of wearing bells. "Peter, eat your peas. In the first place, we've already accepted, and in the second place, the admiral has contacts here that could be useful to your father. And in the third place," she went on before anyone could ask her what she meant, "the Pfeiffers have a lovely home on Coronado Island, just a block or two from the beach. I'm sure you'll all enjoy it if you just make up your minds to."

Meredith decided it didn't sound so bad, after all. Last year they'd spent Thanksgiving with their Harding grandparents and aunts and uncles and a bewildering assortment of cousins—her father came from New England originally. They didn't have any relatives on the West Coast, though, except for some second cousins up in Oregon. Her mother's parents lived in Texas and would be coming for Christmas. By then her father would have shipped out for six months at sea.

To avoid thinking about that, Meredith held out her plate and said, "Could I have some more pot roast, please?" and received an approving look from her mother, who'd asked her earlier if she was feeling all right. Meredith guessed her worry must be showing on her face. She hadn't had a chance yet to tell her parents about the latest poison pen letter, only that she needed to talk to them after dinner.

As he carved Meredith another slice from the roast, Captain Harding said with a grin, "And besides all that, if we weren't going to the Pfeiffers' for Thanksgiving dinner, we'd have to invite the Scofields here." His children groaned, and even his wife's face fell. "Well, they've just arrived in San Diego. Old shipmates, after all."

Peter said indignantly, "Why are the Scofields always following us *around*?"

Meredith knew what he meant. Somehow the families they met and liked in the navy always seemed to get sent to the other end of the country, or even the world, while the ones they didn't like wound up next door. Well, not literally, since the Hardings rarely used base housing, but anyway at the same naval station.

"Hey, it's a small ocean," Captain Harding teased. "Can I help it if the Scofields keep crossing our bow?"

A small ocean, a small world. Meredith was suddenly no longer hungry for the savory bite of meat she'd been about to take. She put down her fork, thinking how her own world seemed to have shrunk to just seven people, at least one of whom was most definitely someone she'd never choose as a shipmate, not to mention a friend.

CHAPTER 13

"Looks like the place isn't even open yet," Dan observed as he cruised his new-old Mazda into the zoo parking lot. "You guys sure you want to be here this early?"

"That's the whole idea," Corky told him, bouncing up and down on the peeling backseat—she was in a really hyper mood this morning. "It'll be real quiet for about an hour," she explained, "and that makes the animals *different,* you know? Like they're sort of peaceful, but more alive, too— not turned off like they get when there's a whole bunch of people staring at them. And today it's gonna get really crowded later on, because of Thanksgiving and all the tourists."

"A real zoo, you mean," Dan joked. "Well, okay,

but don't climb any fences, no matter how peaceful and quiet the rhinos look."

When he'd let them off in front of the entrance, Meredith understood something of what Corky meant. Without the usual background noise and stir of human activity, the voices of the animals sounded startlingly clear and loud in the still air. It was like listening to a hundred conversations going on at once under the canopy of the eucalyptus leaves: macaws screeching, monkeys chattering, an elephant trumpeting, even a lion roaring hoarsely in the distance.

Early as it was, they weren't the first visitors—there was already a short line outside the ticket booth. Meredith had her own membership card now, so she and Corky were able to bypass the line and go directly through the members' entrance to the turnstiles. No one was tending them yet, and the windows of the gift shops on either side were still shuttered for the night. Even here, though, there was something to see—a flock of salmon-pink flamingos preening and strutting around a shallow pool from which a soft morning mist was still rising.

The air was chilly, making Meredith glad she'd worn her denim jacket. She could tell from the gauzy sunshine that it was going to be a beautiful day—not sharp-edged and brilliant like a Santa Ana day, but radiant and shimmering with invisible moisture from the ocean a few miles away.

While they waited for the turnstiles to open, she and Corky exchanged reports on their respective Thanksgivings.

Dinner at the Pfeiffers' large, Spanish-style house had been a slow and rather formal affair, but afterward they'd gone for a long walk on one of the widest, whitest beaches Meredith had ever seen. The only downer had come when they passed the sprawling Hotel Del Coronado with its tennis courts and terraces and conical red roofs. Meredith had thought of Mrs. Craig and wondered if Dr. Egan had come up with any new ideas about the identity of the poison pen writer. She herself had said nothing to anyone about her suspicions of Sara, knowing that was all they were—suspicions.

Corky's Thanksgiving dinner, by contrast, had been a couple of tamales and a frozen-custard cone bought from a street vendor in Tijuana, just over the border in Mexico.

"My dad and I decided a long time ago that we didn't need to do a lot of boring family stuff on Thanksgiving," she said with a shrug. "I mean, sitting around a table with a bunch of relatives . . . who needs it? Also, Paula hates cooking things like turkeys and sweet potatoes. The one time she tried it, the sweet potatoes weren't done all the way through and she forgot to make any gravy and we all just sat there *chewing,* you know?"

As Meredith laughed, Corky went on, "So now we always go out somewhere and spend money. Well, that's one way of giving thanks, right? And then we came home and I read Will all his favorite bedtime stories while Dad and Paula went to some jazz concert up in Del Mar."

For a moment Corky's face seemed to cloud over, making Meredith wonder if she might not secretly miss having a regular Thanksgiving, whatever she said. She seemed restless, too, flipping her plastic zoo card rapidly back and forth between her fingers. Meredith saw that her nails were rimmed with green, almost the same dark green as the hooded sweatshirt she was wearing. She wouldn't put it past Corky to experiment with green nail polish, even to match an old sweatshirt, but decided it was probably paint instead. Corky must have gotten up early, as she sometimes did, to use the studio for an hour or so before Paula started work.

In fact, Corky looked sort of tired, with dark smudges under her eyes. When she pushed back the hood of her sweatshirt, her hair was even crinklier than usual, as if she'd forgotten to brush it that morning.

At last an attendant appeared to unlock the turnstiles.

"All *right!*" Corky said, her mood ebullient again as he let them through. To Meredith's surprise, though, she turned to the right instead of heading straight for the gorilla exhibit, as Meredith had resignedly expected she would.

"The really neat place this time of day is up with the giraffes and antelopes and things," Corky explained, leading the way along a shady walk past a café and a water garden. "There's hardly anyone around, and you can almost pretend you're in Africa." She frowned. "Anyway, I'm not sure I even want to look at the gorillas today. It's so sad about Moke."

Moke was the baby gorilla that Corky and thousands of other visitors doted on. A few weeks earlier, his mother, Amina, had suddenly refused to feed him or groom him or even let him near her, for reasons no one understood. There'd been articles about it in the newspaper, with experts offering opinions and advice. Now the keepers were trying to get Moke to bond with one of the other adult females, so far with little success.

Meredith was about to say something in sympathy, but Corky's mood had changed again. She stopped beside the kookaburra cage next to the walk, nudged Meredith in the ribs, and began singing the old song in a loud, uninhibited voice:

Kookaburra sits in the old gum tree,
Merry, merry king of the bush is he.
Laugh, kookaburra, laugh, kookaburra . . .

She broke off, shaking her head. "Darn, I never can get that bird to say *anything,* never mind laugh."

"Maybe you scare him," Meredith said with a grin as the big bird glared at Corky with its baleful, reddish eye. Corky was all too right when she said she couldn't carry a tune.

They were moving on when Meredith thought of something.

"Oh, hey," she said, stopping short. "I'd better call my dad, to remind him about picking us up on his way home." Her family was driving them both ways today, since Paula had already done more than her share of chauffeuring. Remembering that they'd passed some phone booths back by the main restrooms, Meredith told Corky to go ahead. "I'll catch up in a couple of minutes. Meet you by the giraffes, okay?"

"Okay," Corky agreed, and set off again with her springy stride. She even had paint on her shoe,

Meredith noticed, fishing in her pocket to make sure she had enough change for the call. Corky must be working on one of the oversized canvases Paula had been letting her use lately, the bigger the better.

Back at the phone booths, Meredith called home and was surprised when her mother answered on the second ring. She'd planned to be out most of the day at some naval relief function. Her father was on leave over the Thanksgiving weekend but had an appointment downtown later that morning. He'd been in the shower when Meredith left, and she'd forgotten to leave him a note.

"Oh, Meredith, I'm so glad you called," her mother said, sounding unusually agitated. "I went over to the Edwards' as soon as I heard, but then I thought I'd better come back here in case Corky changed her mind and wanted a ride home. Is she all right? I hope she isn't too upset."

"Why would she be upset?" Meredith said blankly.

"You mean she didn't tell you?" There was a baffled pause before Mrs. Harding said, "Someone broke into Paula's studio last night and vandalized it—destroyed the new series of paintings she's been working on, and most of the sculptures, too." As Meredith stood stunned, she went on, "They've had the police and the insurance adjuster there, all kinds of people milling about. You must have noticed the cars when you picked Corky up."

Meredith shook her head, forgetting that her mother couldn't see her. Corky had been waiting on the corner for them, standing on tiptoe and waving, so Dan hadn't even driven past the house.

"I can't imagine why Corky wouldn't have said something," Joyce Harding said. "I mean, it's not exactly your everyday kind of happening, and Paula is pretty devastated. Some kind of crank, the police think—possibly someone who saw her work in an exhibit and had some kind of weird reaction to it and tracked her down. Whoever it was left a message on that big window at the back, these huge letters in green paint . . ."

She hesitated. "I'd just as soon not repeat what it said, but it was extremely unpleasant. In fact, I'm surprised Corky wanted to go to the zoo today at all, she and Paula are so close. Paula said she'd urged her to go ahead, but still . . . I gather Corky didn't hear anything last night, even though her room is at that back corner of the house. And of course they can't start cleaning up until the police are through."

She went on to describe the mess in the studio, how the vandal had used a razor blade to slash the canvases and something like a hammer to smash the sculptures.

Meredith barely listened. Her mind seemed to have frozen over at the words "message" and "green paint." The paint on Corky's shoe was green, like the paint around her fingernails. A razor blade . . . She saw Corky flipping her zoo card from hand to hand, saw the tiny nicks on the ball of her right thumb and the narrow red line of a fresh cut in the fleshy part of her palm.

When she tuned back in, her mother was saying with a sigh, "Well, I suppose Corky's just trying to put the whole thing out of her mind for a few hours—and I know how much she loves the animals. I don't know, Meredith, maybe it's best if you don't say anything to her for now. Don't let on you know what's happened, I mean."

"She thinks I'm calling Dad down at the naval station," Meredith said slowly, realizing that was what Corky would have assumed—she hadn't explained that he had the day off.

"Meredith?" Her mother had caught something in her tone. "Are you all right? Listen, hon, don't worry about it too much—it was a horrible thing to have happen, but Paula's pretty tough, you know, and I'm sure they'll catch the person who did it."

"I'm sure they will, too," Meredith told her.

"Listen, Mom, I've got to go now. Talk to you later."

She hung up without saying good-bye and took off at a run, using the main walkway instead of the path she and Corky had taken earlier. She barely noticed the elephants looming on her left as she pounded past, nor the long-tailed colobus monkeys on her right, leaping and playing in their airy cage.

There seemed to be no thought in her mind at all, only pictures. Corky painting a message on a window . . . and before that, Corky sitting at the worktable in her room with scissors and paste, carefully snipping and trimming . . . Corky at the computer in her father's study, tapping out a name and an address.

As she ran past the camels and gazelles and headed into the curve leading to the zoo's upper level, she almost collided with another runner, a bearded young guy in jogging clothes. He grinned at her as he dodged aside. "Great place for a workout, right?" he called over his shoulder, running on.

At the top, the roadway leveled out. Meredith stopped to catch her breath and get her bearings among the maze of intersecting paths that wound between the enclosures. Which way to the giraffes? A zoo sign nearby showed profiles of animal heads, including a giraffe's, but Meredith wasn't sure just which way it was pointing.

Never mind, she thought bitterly. There was no way she could miss something as tall and obvious as a giraffe, even if she'd managed to miss the fact that it was her own good friend Corky—blithe, outgoing Corky, everyone's friend, in fact—who had been responsible all along for the poison pen letters.

CHAPTER 14

Corky was watching the tallest of the giraffes nibble on an acacia branch. Her hands were stuffed into the center pocket of her sweatshirt, and her hair gleamed like copper wire in the sunlight. Near her was a plump middle-aged woman, oddly dressed in a summery pastel skirt and blouse, with some kind of shiny hat perched on top of her head.

As Meredith slowed to a walk, her heart pounding, words starting to crowd up into her throat, she saw that Corky was trying to edge away from the woman, who seemed to be talking to both Corky and the giraffes.

"Now this one I call Angela," she said in a crooning voice. "Just look at those eyes, what I call a melting gaze . . . isn't she a darling? Unlike Dorcas here, who has quite a temper, I'm afraid." The hat was a child's party hat, Meredith saw now, made of silver foil with a pink rosette stapled to the brim.

Corky turned, caught sight of Meredith, and hurried toward her with a broad grin of relief.

"I thought you'd never get here," she said, rolling her eyes at the woman behind her. "I told you there were always some crazies here first thing in the morning."

"Crazies," Meredith repeated. She stood staring at her friend through a haze of anger and grief and bewilderment. "You're the one that's crazy, Corky. You're the one that's been doing all the poison pen letters. And now Paula—" She choked up. "Why would you want to hurt Paula, when she's always been so great to you?"

Corky had gone still at Meredith's first words.

"So you found out," she said, and shrugged. "Well, no big deal. I mean, they were only letters, right? Some people just can't take a joke."

Meredith shook her head. "They weren't jokes, Corky. You know they weren't."

"I guess I should've expected it," Corky went on, as though Meredith hadn't spoken, "the way you're always sneaking around. Oh, I've seen how you watch people, Meredith—how you're always listening to them and trying to find out their secrets. You and old Graybags, having your sneaky little conferences after school, thinking you're so smart."

Her tone was so vicious that Meredith took an involuntary step backward.

But now Corky's expression changed again, clouding over the way it had earlier, a look of confusion replacing the anger of a moment ago. "I didn't wreck Paula's studio, though." She shook her head vehemently. "Someone else did that. I wouldn't do anything that mean to Paula, even though she isn't my mother."

Meredith grabbed Corky's hand and held it up in front of her face. "Corky, look—green paint. And green paint on your shoe."

Corky stared down at her shoe, frowning. Then she wrenched her hand away, spun around, and ran.

Shaken by the momentary look of anguish on Corky's face, Meredith hesitated for a moment, then ran after her.

Corky had taken a steep, curving path that led to an amphitheater used for special shows. It was deserted now, and so was the shadowy canyon below, a remote part of the zoo with only a few exhibits lining its rocky walls.

Halfway down, the path angled around a small

rest area furnished with a drinking fountain and a stone bench set back against the metal fence. Here Corky stopped and turned, so abruptly that Meredith almost ran into her.

"You don't need to know about the letters," she said in a flat voice, backing up against the water fountain. "I don't *want* you to know."

"Corky, please, I just want to understand. If I could understand, maybe I could help."

Corky seemed to consider this for a moment. Then she shook her head. "You'll tell everyone." Her face was pale and set, her freckles like a spatter of dried blood across her cheekbones.

"No, I won't, I promise. No one knows about the last two letters anyway, except for me and Ms. Gray and—"

"You'll tell Jeff," Corky interrupted. "Oh, you think you're the only one that notices things, but I've seen you hanging around Jeff, trying to get him away from me. Well, you can just forget it."

She gave Meredith a sudden shove that sent her stumbling against the corner of the bench.

"Just go away, Meredith. You're not my friend anymore, so just go away!"

Corky was shouting in her face now, crowding Meredith back against the railing, gripping her elbows. The cold metal pressed into Meredith's spine. There was a sheer drop on this side of the path, down into a dark ravine tangled with vines and saplings and sharp with broken rocks.

Meredith strained against Corky's weight, trying to turn her shoulders sideways. Out of control, she thought numbly, remembering Ms. Gray's words. Last night in Paula's studio, and now—

"No, no!" called a high-pitched voice somewhere above them. "Bad girls, fighting in the zoo! It upsets the animals, even when they can't see you. Why, poor Angela is positively trembling!"

The giraffe lady stood at the top of the path, peering anxiously down at them, her birthday hat glinting absurdly in the sunlight.

With a strangled sound that might have been a laugh or a sob, Corky released her grip on Meredith. A moment later, she was running away again, fleeing down the path into the canyon.

When Meredith found her twenty minutes later, Corky was sitting on one of the benches overlooking the gorilla exhibit. Of course, Meredith thought tiredly—I should have known.

She'd tried Bear Canyon in one direction, then the sea lion pool in the other, where people sat at sunny tables, laughing and clapping at the antics of the swift, sleek animals. She'd gone partway into the canyon that housed the big cats and met the cold, unblinking stare of the Siberian tiger pacing its rocky enclosure, watched in silence by a few visitors who stood well back from the railing, parents holding the hands of their children. Corky wasn't among them.

Finally, she'd climbed back up to the zoo's main level through the tropical aviary, taking none of her usual pleasure in the rippling stream that made shadowy pools among the giant ferns, or in the bright birds flashing through the glossy foliage about her.

How could she have thought the poison pen writer was Sara Freeman? Sara scowled and complained and said rude things; when she got really mad, she took a punch at someone. She didn't store up anger inside herself, to be let out silently and stealthily, like tapping a toxic gas that was invisible and odorless until the moment of its release.

She should have remembered that she was looking for someone who wasn't what she seemed, Meredith thought bleakly, ignoring a crowned pigeon preening itself on the branch of a fig tree nearby—someone whose rage was hidden beneath smiles and chatter and laughter. Someone like Corky.

Corky, who now sat motionless, staring at the gorillas across the way while tears rolled slowly down her cheeks. Meredith saw that she was alone on the bench, as if other people too had seen something wrong and unnatural about her—as if she were someone to be shunned, like the giraffe lady, Meredith thought, her own eyes stinging suddenly.

"Corky?" she said tentatively.

Corky didn't even turn her head when Meredith sat down beside her. She'd pulled up the hood of her green sweatshirt, and Meredith couldn't see her expression, only the unnatural fixity of her profile and the glistening path of the tears that slid unchecked over her freckled cheekbone.

Meredith drew in her breath. "I think we should go home now, Corky," she said carefully. "I'll go call my mom. Okay?"

Corky didn't respond. Instead she said in a toneless voice, still staring straight ahead, "Even his grandmother won't go near him anymore. Did you know that?"

Meredith turned to look at the gorillas. Moke, the baby gorilla, she must mean—but Meredith didn't see him anywhere. As for the adults, Meredith couldn't tell them apart, the way Corky could, and had no idea which of the older females might be Moke's grandmother.

She met the somber gaze of a large silverback male sitting on a rock ledge with his arms folded across his massive chest. Feeling the familiar twinge of pity and guilt, Meredith dropped her eyes quickly and turned back to Corky.

But Corky had nothing more to say, it seemed. She continued to stare and made no move to wipe away the tears. When Meredith found a clean tissue in her jacket pocket and put it into Corky's hand, her fingers curved around it, but that was all. Meredith saw that she had gone far away, somewhere deep inside herself where Meredith couldn't follow.

Corky had been right about the zoo's getting crowded as the day went on. It took Meredith a long time to get to a phone, working her way against a tide of strolling, laughing family groups. She didn't think she had to worry about Corky's running away again, though. Somehow she knew that Corky had already run as far as she could.

CHAPTER 15

"I still don't understand," Meredith told Paula the next day. "How could Corky write the letters and not know *why* she was writing them?"

"Anger," Paula said simply. "A whole lot of anger she couldn't admit to feeling." She shook her head. "I blame myself, in a way. Here I thought I was doing such a great job as a stepmother, and all the time I never really thought how Corky must feel at having been abandoned by her own mother."

It was early afternoon, and they were sitting in Corky's sunny bedroom, Paula on the window seat and Meredith on the end of the bed. At their feet, two small black cats tumbled and capered—the Lesters' unwanted kittens, acquired as a coming-home present for Corky. Mr. Edwards had called from the hospital a few minutes before to say that Corky was sleeping now and that the doctors thought they'd be able to release her in the morning.

Meredith said, "I don't see how you could have known, the way Corky always seemed so happy and cheerful, like nothing could ever really bother her. And if she didn't know she was angry, not even when she was doing the letters . . . "

"Ah, but that was the other Corky," Paula said sadly. "The one she couldn't admit to being."

Meredith hesitated a moment, then said, "Corky really did have a headache, you know, during the Santa Ana."

Paula nodded. "Yes. The doctors say outside factors like the weather can sometimes trigger these episodes."

For as Corky had described it to her father and the doctor at the hospital, the need to write the letters always began with a kind of headache—a feeling of pressure and darkness inside her head, as if walls were closing in on her and she couldn't breathe.

If the pressure got bad enough, Corky would stop trying to resist it. Instead, she would flatten herself against one of the black walls (that was how she thought of it) and let the other Corky take over. She would watch this person compose her message of hatred—taking her time about it, smiling slyly to herself as she cut and pasted, as she licked a stamp and pressed it on the envelope, as she dropped the envelope into the corner mailbox on her way to the school bus stop the next morning.

And then it would be the old Corky who emerged into the sunlight, lighthearted once more, calling jokes and greetings to her friends as she scrambled aboard the bus and slid into the seat someone had saved for her.

"But the people she chose," Meredith said slowly. "The women she sent the letters to . . . " She shook her head. "I still don't get that."

Paula picked up a worn photograph from the cushion beside her and handed it to Meredith. "I found this hidden at the back of Corky's closet," she said. "Under the magazines and newspapers. Mothers, don't you see? Young mothers."

As Meredith studied the picture, Paula asked, "Is there any real resemblance? To Mrs. Norman, I mean? I never had a chance to meet her. And to the other younger woman—the gym teacher with the little girl?"

Meredith looked at the smiling young woman in the photo. Corky had that same smile, the same feathery, flyaway eyebrows. "Not really," she said. "Except they're both blond and pretty too, I guess."

She struggled to make sense of what Paula had just said. "But Corky told me she didn't mind about her mother leaving. She understood about her being young and needing to live her own life. I mean, she didn't *hate* her."

Paula sighed. "What Corky said and what she really felt underneath were two different things, I'm afraid." Absently, she nudged one of the kittens with her toe. It rolled over and grasped her shoe in its tiny claws. "The older women who got the letters . . . in their sixties, you said, and thin and wiry, with glasses? And both with grandchildren?"

Meredith nodded.

"Like Alma Jarvis, then." When Meredith looked at her blankly, Paula explained, "Corky's grandmother—her mother's mother. Who also abandoned her."

Heartsick, Meredith remembered Corky's remark at the zoo about the gorilla baby, made in that strange, flat, hopeless voice. No wonder she'd been fixated on Moke, rejected by his mother and grandmother, too.

It was the last thing Corky said for almost twelve hours—which must have been some kind of record for Corky, Meredith thought, though the idea didn't make her want to smile. Paula and Mr. Edwards had taken her to the hospital in midafternoon. There she'd allowed herself to be examined and undressed and settled in bed without a word, still with those spooky tears rolling slowly down her cheeks.

"Alma isn't a bad woman, really," Paula said. "And Corky acted up a lot with her from what I hear—being really bratty and rebellious. Or maybe I should say she acted out." She thought about that for a moment. "And then, when I came along, Corky pushed all her negative feelings underground. Do you know, she actually threw her arms around me when her father told her we were going to get married?"

She smiled wryly. "I should have known *that* wasn't normal. I mean, what else are ladies' magazines for? But then finally, on Thursday night—or early Friday morning, we're still not sure—she acted out against me."

Troubled by her tone, Meredith said, "But Corky really loves you, Paula. I know she does."

"Maybe. But it's all mixed up with other feelings." When Meredith started to protest, Paula said grimly, "You haven't seen the studio."

The kitten was tugging at Paula's shoelace now. She shook it off gently and leaned back against the window, closing her eyes. Meredith saw with a pang how pale and strained she looked. Even her sheaf of chestnut-brown hair seemed to have lost its healthy gloss.

"I suppose I should be glad things finally came to a head," she said, "so that Corky can get the help she needs. But right now, it's hard to feel that way."

"Corky didn't want to believe it about the studio," Meredith told her, remembering the look of anguish on Corky's face when she'd forced her to look at the green paint. "It was almost like she'd forgotten she'd done it. So maybe it wasn't about hating you so much as—well, sort of needing to hit out and wreck things and make everything be as messed up on the outside as the way she was feeling inside."

Paula opened her eyes. She nodded thoughtfully. "You are a wise child, Meredith," she said. "And you've been a good friend to Corky. Thank heaven you were with her yesterday when she started coming apart."

Meredith hadn't told anyone about Corky's trying to push her over the railing, if that was really what she'd meant to do. Maybe she'd have to if Corky didn't get better from her sessions with the psychiatrist she was going to be seeing after school. But for now, she'd just as soon have that episode stay between her and Corky. Corky might not even remember it, she thought, unless the doctor made her. She hoped that wouldn't have to happen.

The other kitten had been hiding under the bed.

Now it pounced out from under the dust ruffle and sprang at its brother. Or sister? Meredith wasn't sure. Inky or Slinky, anyway, she thought with a smile, remembering Corky's names for them.

Paula smiled too, watching the mock battle. "Only trouble is, they'll grow up to be cats. Sure you won't take one of them?" Before Meredith could answer, her smile faded. "Poor Corky," she said with a shiver. "Talk about growing up . . . Do you know she saved the postcards, too? The ones her mother sent after she ran away. Just a handful of them, saying things like 'It's so pretty here at night with all the stars,' and a picture of a desert sunset on the other side. Not even 'I wish you were here.' God! Corky was right to be angry."

Meredith thought about that. "Well, isn't it good now that she knows she is? Angry, I mean?"

Paula nodded. "Yes, I think it's where she has to start." She laughed unexpectedly. "In fact, it's where she started last night, when the dam finally burst. Did I tell you she threw a can of talcum powder at one of the nurses? Luckily, she missed."

Meredith grinned. As she knew from trying to play whiffleball with Corky, her aim wasn't much truer than her singing voice.

"You know, I just realized something," Paula said, sitting up straight. "The first two doctors Corky saw couldn't get anything out of her. Then Dr. Wheeler came on duty—a young woman doctor with, get this, blond hair and a nice smile. Corky wasn't any more responsive with her than she'd been with the others until she—Dr. Wheeler—was paged and stood up to leave the room. She said something about how she'd be right back, and then . . . well, that was when Corky suddenly started yelling and throwing things and crying—real tears, I mean, not those creepy silent ones—like a little kid having a tantrum."

Meredith said slowly, "As if her mother was leaving all over again. Is that what you mean?"

Paula nodded. "Her mother might even have said that, too—'I'll be right back.' Only she never returned."

CHAPTER 16

They were both silent for a long moment. The kittens had fallen asleep on the rug, tangled together in a pool of sunlight that made their black fur glisten.

"Anyway," Paula said, "it was after that that Corky began talking. Nonstop all night, from what her father said. Poor man, he must be exhausted. At least I got a few hours sleep." She sighed. "It's been a terrible shock for him, finding out how mixed up Corky's been inside. I don't think he realized until now just how much she means to him."

Meredith said hesitantly, "Well, that's another good thing, isn't it? In fact, it looks like a lot of good things might come out of this. And it's not like

Corky's alone, with no one to care about her. She has her father and you and Will and all her friends."

She paused. She was pretty sure the kids at school wouldn't have to know about the letters—that would be between Corky and Ms. Gray and Mr. Leonard. But how would they react when they found out Corky'd had a sort of breakdown and was having to see a shrink, as they'd put it? Well, she thought, if anyone could carry it off, Corky could.

"And there's her talent, too—her art."

Paula smiled. "Except that she doesn't really have any. Oh, I know I've encouraged her, she was so enthusiastic, but Corky still can't draw a hand that looks any different from a foot." She sobered again. "Maybe that was wrong of me. Yes, I know it was. I was dealing with Corky-on-the-surface, I guess, the way we've all been doing for so long. Too long."

A faint wail sounded from down the hall. "Sounds like nap time is over," Paula said, getting to her feet. She pondered a moment. "You know, in spite of everything, I think I can honestly say that Corky's never been jealous of Will. Bless her heart for that."

She left to tend to Will. Meredith sat looking around the colorful, messy room. Reflected light from the swimming pool danced on the ceiling and on the posters that plastered the walls, some of them overlapping. Corky could never bear to throw a poster away, any more than she could bear to part with even the most threadbare of the stuffed animals that crowded her headboard and dresser and spilled over onto the bookcase.

Most people would have said the room looked just like Corky, Meredith thought, right down to the tumble of shoes and jeans and sweatshirts inside the open closet door—an innocent, ordinary clutter that gave no hint of the cache that had lain behind it, hidden in the far corner: the tidy stack of magazines and newspapers, the envelopes and stamps, the scissors that were identical to the pair in the mug on Corky's worktable but that had been reserved for one special purpose.

Meredith swallowed hard. She thought how shocked Ms. Gray was going to be when Mr. Edwards called her and told her that Corky was the poison pen writer. But maybe not. Remembering how Ms. Gray had never seemed to warm to Corky the way most people did, Meredith thought maybe she'd sensed all along that there was more to Corky than met the eye—that there were depths of shadow beneath her bright surface.

And the shadow part of Corky had known that, Meredith thought suddenly. It was why she'd never been at ease with Ms. Gray, why she'd resorted to jibes and name-calling behind her back, using them like shields against the teacher's clear, perceptive gaze.

One of the kittens mewed in its sleep and was answered by the other. Meredith stirred them with her toe, but they only stretched and blinked and dozed off again. Corky was right, she thought—it would be a shame to separate them, especially now that Paula seemed resigned to living with two kittens underfoot. Maybe she wouldn't offer to take one, after all.

And anyway, she didn't know for sure yet, not absolutely for sure. "Under no circumstances are you to say anything to Peter," her mother had warned. "Not until it's official. We're only telling you now because of Corky. You look like you could use some cheering up, and . . . well, we thought it might help to know you have more of a stake here than you thought."

Because suddenly, astonishingly, it looked as though her family might be staying in San Diego for good. Captain Harding had been offered a job with one of the big defense corporations that was in the process of converting its Cold War technology to other uses. The job would be something of a gamble, since down-sizing was bound to be part of the process. Still, he'd just about decided to retire from the navy when his current tour of duty was up.

"I'm tired of being a rolling stone," he'd said. "A *wet* rolling stone that doesn't even gather moss, just barnacles."

In spite of his joking tone, Meredith thought he would miss the navy. She couldn't help worrying that he might be taking a civilian job mainly because of her and Lindsay and Peter—and Dan too, of course, though he'd be going away to college next year.

When she'd voiced this worry to her mother, though, Joyce Harding had surprised her by saying crisply, "Well, and why not? A good crew, years of loyal service . . . seems to me we've earned a home port, myself included." In a softer tone, she'd added, "Your father's missed a lot of your growing up, you know. There aren't that many more years when we'll all be together as a family. He wants to be part of that."

Meredith tried to imagine having an address that didn't change every few years—and not only a state and city address, a street address, too. Her parents were talking about buying the house they were renting, provided the owner named a reasonable price. In any case, they were determined to stay on in the same neighborhood so their schools wouldn't change.

She thought about having the same friends right on through high school: Virginia and Emily and Connie and Jeff and Pete—even Noah Wright and Sara and Deirdre and mousy Mary Lee Mumford.

And of course Corky. Meredith felt close to Corky now in a way she'd never imagined she would. But would Corky feel the same way about her? Or would she try to put a distance between them, out of an uncomfortable feeling that Meredith knew things about her that no one else did?

There was Jeff, too. Could she and Corky still be friends if it turned out it was Meredith that Jeff liked?

It was hard to imagine Corky backing off from anyone or anything. Still . . .

As Meredith slid off the bed and looked around for her denim jacket—things had a way of disappearing into the scenery in Corky's room—she heard Will scampering down the hall.

"Kitties!" he exclaimed, arriving in the doorway with his arms outstretched. He saw Meredith and beamed at her. "Hi, Merry," he said, pronouncing the "r's" like "w's." He rushed past her to squat down beside the sleeping kittens.

Meredith smiled wryly. Well, Meredith *was* kind of a long name for a little kid to say, she conceded. She'd just have to keep working on Will as he grew up.

And she'd keep working on Corky, too. Because she herself wasn't going to back off, not if she was finally going to have a real home and a real stake in things. Just as Corky might be free at last to be a whole person, someone who felt hurt and anger as well as laughter and warmth and joy in living, so Meredith would be free to be her own changeable self from one day to the next—Meredith Harding, who was sometimes grumpy, who sometimes disappeared for hours to read a book or play her flute, who sometimes turned in sloppy homework, who sometimes even goofed off in class.

The minute she knew for sure that they were staying, she thought, Corky would be the first person she'd tell.

Author's Note

The story of Moke, the baby gorilla, is my own invention, though such occurrences are not uncommon among the great apes, whether in the wild or in captivity. (I like to think that Moke has since been adopted by a loving stepmother and her family!)

Like all great zoos, the San Diego Zoo is constantly expanding and upgrading its facilities. Thus readers who visit it may notice some changes in the placement of exhibits since this book was written.